GEM OF RESILIENCY

CAMILLE MICHAELS

This is a work of fiction. Names, characters, businesses, places, events, and incidents are either the products of the author's imagination or used in a fictitious manner. Any resemblance to actual persons, living or dead, or actual events is purely coincidental.

ISBN: 978-1-7356416-4-5

DEDICATION

To everyone who lives everyday with anxiety. You are warriors.

CHAPTER ONE

Slamming the closet door, I put my hands on my hips, sigh heavily, tilt my head back, and let out a tiny scream.

This is ridiculous, I think to myself.

Calm down. It will be okay.

It will not!

Whoa. You're feisty for a Monday morning.

That's because I have to go into the office. I haven't been to the office on a Monday in months, and it has been glorious.

Yes, it has. But you used to go into the office five days a week, remember?

Ew. I try to not remember those dark days. Carl gave me permission to work from home on Monday and Friday. Why is he making me go in today? It's not right.

He said there was a meeting you need to attend. That's why.

Well, I don't like it. I've grown accustom to working in leggings on Mondays. It's a nice way to ease into the week. I don't have to see anyone. All of my meetings are over the phone. They don't even make me go on video. I'm sure they don't want to see me, as well.

Who would want to when you look like that?

Ugh. I can't have coffee today, either. I have a couple meetings, not to mention the super-secret one that Carl is forcing me to come in to attend. I don't need to be a caffeinated freakshow for whatever shit gets lobbed my way in that meeting.

Way to be optimistic, Gemma.

Just keeping it real. My track record for being normal in meetings is zero.

Zero? There has to have been one in which you weren't weird.

Nothing is coming to mind.

What about…? How about…?

See.

I slip on my high heels, straighten my sweater, brush the lint off my pants, and run my hands over my brown hair as I peek one more time in the mirror. My tired, green eyes are staring back at me. Grabbing my purse, I take a longing glance at my studio apartment and my coffeemaker before closing the door and heading out of my apartment building.

It's autumn in Boston. Leaves cover the sidewalks and streets. Those left on the trees are barely hanging on. It is dark and chilly in the mornings. Daylight Savings ends in a couple of weeks, so soon it will be dark by four in the afternoon.

Walking through the door to Sally's coffeeshop, I see my two favorite guys standing side by side at the counter in front of Sally. She grins when she sees me. Beautiful smile lines crease her mouth and forehead and just next to her eyes. Her auburn, slightly greying, hair is pulled back into a ponytail at the bottom of her neck.

"Hey, Sweetie," she says to me.

McGruff and Walter both turn around.

"Hey, beautiful," McGruff says as he steps forward, wraps his arm around my waist, and kisses the top of my head. His baby blue eyes look into mine as he sweeps his light brown hair out of them.

When I met him, his hair was short, almost spikey, but it has grown a good amount in the last few months, so he has to flip it around to get it out of his vision. He has kept his beard short and wrapped around his square jaw.

You know, one day, you may want to start referring to him as Nate, you know, his real name.

Nah. He will always be McGruff to me.

McGruff is what I nicknamed him before we met, when I'd see him around the office building or the park nearby, and he'd gruffly say, "Hi," and then walk away.

And you acted awkwardly and ran in the opposite direction.

2

Yeah, it's a wonder he liked me.

Still is, honestly.

"Hey, kid," Walter says. "I'm going to miss our coffee time this morning."

"Me too."

Walter is in his eighties and walks and stands bent over from back pain. He lives down the hall from me in my apartment building and has been keeping me company on Monday mornings. He brings me coffee from Sally's as I lazily scroll through my emails and wake up to the prospect of a brand-new week. I look forward to his visit every Monday. It has been a while since I looked forward to a Monday, but now it seems almost natural.

Natural? To look forward to a Monday?

Oh, shut up. I needed this in my life. My Mondays with Walter are great. And today it is being ripped from me.

Still being dramatic, are you? Calm down. It's just one day. It's not like Carl is taking all the Mondays at home away from you.

He'd better not!

Girl, you need to chill. Breathe, please.

I take a breath.

"What can I get for you, Sweetie?" Sally asks me.

"A hot tea, please."

"You got it."

When I am in the office, I try to eliminate coffee from my diet to avoid my anxiety worsening, especially in meetings.

You also eliminate caffeine jitters.

And happiness.

Again, with the drama.

"What's so important at work today?" Walter asks me.

Walter has somehow become one of my best friends over the last few years. Rarely do I notice that he is over fifty years my senior.

"I wish I knew," I answer.

Maybe you're getting fired.

Stop it. I'm not. Am I?

No, he'd definitely do that on a Friday.

Good point. I will wait on boxing up my desk, then.

Yeah, that would be a little premature, Gemma, considering it's a department meeting. I don't think he'd call you out to be fired in front of everyone.

Unless we're all getting fired.

Oh, my God, Gemma. You're not that lucky.

"Well, I, for one, am glad that I get to walk in with you this morning," McGruff says.

I smile up at him.

After a little rough patch a couple of months ago, McGruff and I have gotten a lot closer. I feel more comfortable sharing my feelings about anxiety with him, and he also shares his with me. I was quite irritable and hard to be around before my medication was switched. Since it has been, I feel a lot better. My mind is less stressed, and I actually feel more like myself again. McGruff has been really understanding and open to learning about my anxiety and responses. If I run away, he knows whether to let me be or to follow. I think Walter had some influence on that reaction, too. Walter's wife, according to his son, Josh, was a lot like me. I think McGruff tried to pick his brain a little. The three of us have even been going to senior tai chi together Saturday mornings at Frog Pond at the Boston Common.

"The only good thing about going to the office," I reply. "That and seeing Sally, of course."

"All right. Here's your tea," Sally says. "Now, get out of here before you make me blush."

I smile at her, look at Walter, and say, "Bye, Walter."

He winks at me as he turns to take a seat at one of the tables by the window. The café only has four tables. I smile to myself as I remember sitting at a different table than McGruff when he had the audacity to want to have lunch with me when we first met. The door dings as McGruff and I walk out into the crisp morning air.

4

"Don't pout," McGruff says to me.

"I'm not pouting," I retort. McGruff raises his eyebrows. "I'm scowling."

"Then don't scowl. You used to go into the office every day, remember?"

"Yes, I remember. I vividly remember the agony of five days in the office."

"Okay, there. I think someone is missing her best friend today."

"Liz?"

"I meant coffee."

Foolish man. Coffee is not my best friend. It is my one true love.

Don't tell him that!

I won't. Just like I will never tell him that I secretly call him McGruff.

I giggle. "I guess I am over reacting a little."

"Don't worry, my Gemma," he says and puts his arm around my shoulders. "We will get through this day."

"Just as we always do."

My light-hearted cheerfulness ends when the elevator doors close on McGruff's blue eyes looking back at me, and I am left alone in the box. I grumpily step over the slit of death, walk past my coworkers, and sit with a thud at my desk.

Try to relax, Gemma. Being in the office isn't that bad.

No, I don't think I will relax. Not that I even have a choice. My body chooses for me. And it always chooses anxiety.

I work at KPM Insurance Company. It is a mid-sized insurance company based in Boston. I have yet to figure out what KPM stands for even though I've worked here for almost five years. We are in the process of overhauling our administration system, which is transitioning from an old green-screen mainframe to a modern web-based site for all administration and claim tasks. Being a business analyst, or BA, in IT, I am mostly focused on creating requirements and making sure that everyone on project teams, meaning the programmers, have all the information that they need to complete the project. I was on the project team for Bookroll, which is our nickname for the part of the project that rolled all of our policies from the mainframe to the web-based system, and I had to attend daily torture, I mean status, meetings. But thankfully, Carl said I no longer had to attend them because the requirements were finished. I still have nightmares about the meetings and cringe every time the word Bookroll is mentioned. I live in constant fear that I will be pulled back into the daily meetings, most notably because my nemesis, Jack, is in them.

Can you really still call him your nemesis if you never interact with him anymore?

Yes. I definitely can. Does one ever lose nemesis status? Is it a 'til-death-do-you-part type of thing?

Honestly, not sure how that works.

Maybe someday, but today is not that day.

Being in the office on a day I am not supposed to be has increased my irritability and hostility to my coworkers at an exponential rate. There is the throat clearer clearing his throat from across the office. There is the woman who always takes conference calls on speaker so we can all hear her yelling into the phone as well as both sides of the argument. There is the sneezer, who sneezes not once, not twice, but at least three times in a row at such a high-pitched decibel that it is one level below the pitch only dogs can hear. There is the pen tapper, who is constantly tapping his pen against his desk. And last, but not least, there is Barb who is loudly, open-mouth, chewing and snapping gum a couple cubicles behind mine.

Calm down, Gemma. It's just the normal office building sounds.

I shouldn't be hearing any of it! I should be home.

It's okay. Just breathe.

It's not okay. I'd flip my desk if it weren't bolted to the ground and attached to every other desk in this row.

Although that would be quite a sight, why don't you put on your headphones and listen to some calming music? Stacey did recommend that you listen to music during the day. Listen to your therapist's advice.

I can do that. But what if people know that I put on the headphones to purposefully ignore them?

They won't know. Plus, I'm sure everyone else does the same.

I plug the headphones into my phone and position them over my ears. They are the big ones that look like ear muffs. I don't want anyone to mistake me for someone they can talk to right now. I am off limits.

Who would actually talk to you?

Shut up. People do ask me questions. Carl will check-in sometimes. Brittany talks to me all the time.

Face it. Not even these bulky headphones will keep any of those people from talking to you.

Well, maybe music will at least help me calm down.

I find a classical music station and hit play.

Nope. I'm about to organize a military strike listening to this symphony.

How about some easy pop?

Nope. I can't deal with some girl whining into my ear about some guy.

Okay. What about this relaxing piano station?

Yes. This will do. I just need to get through eight hours sitting in this captivity, that includes my monthly one-on-one meeting with Carl and whatever this super important meeting is that I had to come into this hell hole for today.

Gemma. Calm down. Listen to your relaxing piano. Breathe in. Breathe out. Your negative thinking is just making your anxiety worse.

I lower my chin to my chest, close my eyes, and relax my shoulders.

You've got this. Look at you taking Stacey's advice. She'll be so proud.

Slowly, I take a deep breath in and let it out just as slowly. I can feel my shoulders start to drop and my neck relax.

My phone buzzes. It's a text from McGruff. "How goes it?" it reads.

"Crappy," I respond, pulling my headphones down around my neck. Even calming music can't help.

"It's just one day. You will survive."

I always do.

"True," I respond.

"Now, how are you feeling?"

I, again, type back "crappy" but add a smiley face and hit send.

"That's my girl."

I put down the phone and realize that I am smiling to myself. Damn that McGruff. He can always make me smile.

"Gemma!' A message from Brittany pops up on my computer. "I am so glad you are in the office today!"

"That makes one of us."

"Oh, come on. Nick is happy, too."

"Oh, I'm sure."

I'm sure Nick is happy that the girl he asked out and was flat out rejected by is in the office and sitting two feet from him, only separated by a partition. I am one hundred percent sure that he is not happy about it.

"He is. I just told him you were here."

Great. Why would she do that? I was hoping he'd just not notice me all day, sitting here two feet from him.

"Gemma?" I hear Nick ask through the partition between our desks. "You here?"

God damn it, Brittany.

"No," I respond to him.

"Cool."

"Why did you do that?" I type out to Brittany. "He hates me."

"No, he doesn't. We are a pack, again. Remember?"

I do remember. I just don't believe it.

Every one doesn't hate you, Gemma.

Okay, not everyone. Just Nick.

He has done nothing to make you think that he hates you.

No. He hasn't.

You are a pack, again. Just believe it. You just feel guilty for breaking his little heart.

Not helping.

"Why are you in the office today?" Nick asks through the wall.

"The super-secret meeting this afternoon."

"Carl made you come in for it?"

"Yep."

"Must be big news, then."

"It better be."

I can hear a muffled laugh.

All right, girl. Let's get some work done and sip on this hot tea before it gets cold.

Tea isn't actually that bad. I have actually sort of fallen in love with tea. I mean, it will never be my one true love like coffee, but it ain't that bad. If you buy the right ones, it can be soothing and comforting.

Someone clears his throat across the room, and I roll my eyes up to the ceiling. It's not soothing or comforting enough to block that noise out. I want to march across the floor and throw my tea in that person's face.

Calm the rage just a smidge, would you?

I can't stop. This is who I am now.

Just because your calm Monday was taken away does not mean you are a rage monster now. Just breathe. In and out. You are okay. This is fine. Being in the office is fine. You are fine.

I guess I am fine.

That is right!

"I guess this is fine," I mumble to myself as I start pulling up my spreadsheets.

A few hours pass without any incidents of open hostility or desk flipping. I am left alone with my headphones, listening to relaxing piano until it is time for my monthly one-on-one meeting with my boss Carl. I lock my computer, pick up my notepad, and slowly walk towards the conference room.

He is not sitting at his desk, which is a couple cubicles behind mine, so he is no doubt going to be late. Per usual. I pick a seat at the conference room table, flop my notebook down, and breathe heavily.

"Hey, Gemma!"

I nearly jump out of my seat as Carl greets me and closes the door behind him. He is an African-American man in his sixties, quite tall, and sometimes acts as a father figure. I both like and dislike that attitude towards me. For one, it eases my anxiety and takes a little stress off of me. But on the other hand, I am a grown adult and I don't need someone treating me like a child.

"I am glad you are in the office today, and we get to have this meeting face to face," he says as he sits.

"Me too."

Liar.

"Good. First thing I want to cover is the management conference on Friday."

Okay, so he is going to a conference? No Carl on Friday. Cool.

"Joe had a family emergency," he continues, "so he can't go to the management conference on Friday. I'd like you to take his spot."

Wait. What? I don't understand those words.

"The management conference?" I ask.

"Yes. I'm sorry, I thought you would have heard. It's a conference for professionals who are on the track to becoming management."

Nope. He can't be serious.

"You want *me* to go?"

"Yes. You will be one of six associates going from KPM."

He must've hit his head or something.

"Me?"

"Yes."

He must be hallucinating. There's no way he sees me sitting in front of him and wants me to go to a management conference.

"Okay…"

"Good. It's at Foxwoods."

"The casino?"

"Yes, it is a big place. Have you ever been?"

"No."

"Well, you will be surprised how massive the place is. It has conference areas as well as a bunch of shopping. It's not just a casino."

"Oh, ok."

"It's just for the day. They will give you the schedule when you get there. We've already picked out the presentations for you all to go to. You can probably get a ride with one of the other associates going. It's not too far into Connecticut, so maybe a two-hour drive from here."

"Who else is going?"

"One person from Customer Service, Sales, Product, and Underwriting. And you and Ed from IT."

Is he sure about this? How the hell am I going to get there? No one has a car in Boston. Do they?

"I know Ed is driving," he continues. "You should ask him if you can go with him."

Of course, Ed has a car.

"And next week," he says, "I want to you to take the lead with the state tax issue. I really like this opportunity for you, Gemma. I think you should be on the Project Management track. I have a lot of faith in you."

No. He can't be talking to me.

He used your name.

Then he can't be serious. Me? A project manager?

It's a logical step from business analyst. You just want to be a BA for the rest of your life?

Maybe. I was holding out hope that I would win the lottery or get to be a trophy wife to some rich guy.

"Any questions?"

So many.

"Who in Underwriting is going?"

"Brittany Beauchamp."

That bitch. She didn't tell me about this.

"Okay. And you want me to lead the meetings for the state tax issue?"

"Yes. You can handle that, right?"

I think I might puke.

Of course, you can handle it.

I take a deep breath and say, "Yes, I think I can."

"Good."

No. I am definitely going to barf.

You can do this. You are a warrior princess.

Sure, and if I fail, I will just quit, change my name, move to Ireland, open a pub, and name it Flannery's. Actually, I should do that anyway.

No, you can handle this. You can do anything you put your mind to. You should be proud of yourself for even saying yes to leading the project.

It's a small project, minuscule even.

Even so. Good job for saying yes.

Did I have an option to say no?

Gemma, you can do this. Carl thinks you can do this. You know you can do this. You can do anything. Remember that.

I can. But do I want to?

"How is it working from home?" Carl asks.

Holy crap. I am still in this meeting.

"Do you still like it?" he asks.

"Oh, yes. I do. Very much so. Absolutely."

Way to play it cool, Gemma.

Carl smiles. "Good. Anything else you'd like to talk about while we have the time?"

I think if I talk, I will projectile vomit, so no.

"Not right now."

"Okay, well you know where to find me if you need me. I will send over the information on the conference. Let me know if you have any issues finding a ride."

"Okay."

I don't like this. I don't like this at all. I have to go to a *management* conference, and then I have to lead a project like I am a *manager*.

This is a good thing. It means Carl has a lot of faith in you and wants to give you a great career opportunity.

Yes. But can I handle it?

You can handle anything.

Okay, but do I *want* it?

That is a whole other issue.

Leaving the conference room behind Carl, I walk straight over to Brittany's desk and stand in front of her until she looks up at me. She has short brown hair down to her shoulders and freckles on her nose.

I put my hands on my hips and say, "You didn't tell me about the management conference on Friday."

"I was hoping it wouldn't happen."

"Oh, it's happening. And I'm going with you."

"What!"

"Yep. I got suckered into going by Carl. God knows why he chose me."

"This is going to be so much fun!" Brittany shouts and claps her hands twice.

"It's a management conference," I respond.

"At Foxwoods. Have you ever been?"

"No. Have you?"

"Yes! We should make a weekend of it and stay at least Friday night. Probably Thursday night, too, since it starts Friday morning. What do you think?"

"I don't hate the idea."

"Come on! It will be so much fun!"

You should absolutely do this.

"Oh, okay."

"Yes! I'm so excited now!"

"How are you getting there?" I ask.

"Ugh. Ed is driving me."

"Do you think he'll drive me too?"

"I don't see why not."

"What are you two ladies so excited about?" Nick asks as he appears at my right. Nick is in his early thirties, has straggly brown hair that is always in his face, dark brown eyes, and stubble on his chin, from what I assume is lack of care to shave.

"Gemma is going to the conference on Friday with me. And we're going to stay over!"

"No way! Why am I not invited?"

"You weren't cool enough to get an invite to the conference."

I know what he's thinking: But Gemma was? There's no way I should be going to a management conference. Just listen to those words. Gemma is going to a management conference. It makes no sense. It might as well be gibberish.

"Who else is going?" Nick asks.

"Ed is driving us," Brittany says. "Oh, shit. How are we going to get back if we stay Friday night?"

"Maybe Ed will stay with you," Nick suggests.

"Oh, man. What a drag. I was hoping for a girls' weekend," Brittany says.

"You know Ed won't want to spend any time with us. I think the feeling is mutual. He'd only stick around if Nick was with us," I reply.

14

"True! He and Nick have a bromance."

"Hey! So do the two of you," Nick says.

"Yeah, our bromance is nice," I respond.

Nick fakes a smile. "You know what I mean."

"We could take a bus," I say to change the subject. "I'm sure they have a lot of busses going in and out of there."

"Good point," Brittany says.

"I'm so jealous right now!" Nick exclaims.

"You should be," Brittany replies.

We all go silent as Bob, our VP, walks behind Nick and me. Nick and I smile awkwardly at Brittany and immediately turn to walk back to our desks.

You know, he probably doesn't even care that you are chatting.

Oh, he cares. It is company time.

It's not long before I look up as Brittany stops at my desk, puts her hands in front of her on the partition, and says, "I have good and bad news."

"I'll take the good first."

"We have a ride home from Foxwoods."

"The bad news?"

"It's Ed. He's staying Friday night with us. It'll be okay. We don't have to hang out with him. We don't even have to see him. We'll just pretend he's not there. Don't worry."

"I'm not worried."

You're not?

"You're not?"

"No. It's a big place, so I hear. I'm sure he won't want to see us either."

"Hey, hey, hey ladies," Ed says as he appears by Brittany's side.

Could he sense us talking about him?

"What's up, Ed?" Brittany asks.

"Just excited about our little trippy trip. We are going to have so much fun."

Are you worried now?

Brittany awkwardly smiles and says, "Yeah."

Ed brushes his bushy blonde hair back across his forehead so we can see his hazel eyes. When he was hired a year or so ago, I could have sworn he was only twenty-two years old, based on how he acts, but shortly thereafter, he got married and now has a child. I guess he could still be in his early twenties. Some people do marry young.

"Thanks for driving me, Ed," I say.

"No worries. I was already picking up this gal." He points to Brittany.

"Do you live in Boston?" Brittany asks. "Where do you keep your car?"

"Oh, no. I live in the burbs."

The burbs? Really?

"I know," he says. "You can't picture it. I moved out of the city when I got married. I park my car in my driveway."

"You have a house?" I ask.

I never would have associated Ed with anything related to adulthood.

Gemma, he has wife and a baby.

I know, but I can't picture that at all. How did he hide this part of himself so well?

Behind his immature personality.

Right.

"Yes, Gemma. I have a house. I live the suburban life." Ed smiles, presumably at my incredulous face, and says, "How old do you think I am, Gemma?"

Say twenty-three.

No, that seems too young now. Twenty-five? I don't want to offend him.

Ed doesn't really seem like the type to get offended.

"Twenty-five," I say.

"I'm thirty, Gemma," Ed says, smiles, and walks away.

I slowly turn to Brittany. She has the same look on her face.

"Ed?" she asks. "Our Ed has a house? I mean, I knew he had a wife and a baby, but somehow I didn't think he was living the picket fence life."

"It's definitely a shocker. I kind of always thought he was twenty-two. Never in my life would I have guessed thirty."

"I know! I mean I knew he had a baby, but I somehow never pictured him as a dad."

"Or a grown-up," I quip.

"Yeah…"

"It's hard to take in."

"I still wouldn't worry about him hanging out with us at Foxwoods."

"I'm not."

You're not?

"You're not?" Brittany asks.

"No. Even if we do have to do things with him, he's not that bad. He's not…" I lean in and whisper, "Jack."

"I know you said me," Nick says through the partition. "You don't have to whisper."

"We don't want to hurt your feelings," Brittany responds.

"Any more than you usually do," Nick adds.

"Exactly," Brittany says and smiles. "Toodles," she adds as she walks away.

Nick replaces Brittany in front of my desk and asks, "You ready for the mystery meeting?"

Locking my computer, I stand up and respond, "Yep. It's the reason I'm in the office today, so it'd better be good."

"Or what?" Nick jokes.

"Or…else."

"Or else nothing will change, and you will just go on as you were?"

"Yep."

Nick grins. "Sounds about right."

The meeting is in the largest conference room the company has. It's the only one that can fit the entire IT department. The chairs are lined up in rows and the tables have been removed to make more room. Nick heads to the back row and takes a seat.

Oh, thank goodness. He knows who he is with. If he'd gone to the front, I'd have to ditch him and sit by myself in the back.

Bob is already pacing in front of the room and waiting for the department to file in. There is a woman I've never seen before sitting in the front row with her legs crossed and arms resting casually on her knees. She is wearing a dark blue skirt suit and is very pretty. Long blonde hair is tied in a braid down her back.

Hmm. Mystery woman in a mystery meeting.

Nick leans in to me and asks, "Who is that?"

"Beats me," I whisper back.

"She looks important."

"Maybe she's here to fire all of us."

Nick laughs. "You wish."

"Yeah, I do."

Nick shakes his head. "Well, it's not happening."

Too bad.

"What about some of us? A public shaming and firing all in one?"

Nick looks at me out of the corner of his eye. "How would that work exactly?"

"They call our names, and we have to get up and leave the building immediately. I anticipate tears, maybe even some applause."

Nick shakes his head, again. "You're a strange one, Gemma."

Don't I know it.

Bob looks extra stressed today. Each time he paces back and forth another knot ties itself inside my chest. Would he just sit down already? He's going to give me a panic attack.

Just breathe. Close your eyes if you have to.

And I do. I close my eyes for a split second before Bob clears his throat, and my eyes pop open again.

"Welcome, everyone," he says. "I know this meeting was short notice, but I wanted to get the whole department together so I could tell you all in person before you found out elsewhere."

Oh, shit. We *are* getting fired. They are getting rid of the whole IT department. Holy shit.

Nonsense! They can't. That's impossible.

"It's happening," I whisper to Nick.

I hear him muffle a laugh.

"I just wanted you to hear it from me, that although I love this company and coming here every day and working with all of you, that I am retiring, effective in two weeks."

Whoa. What? I thought he would die here.

Nick turns to look at me. I look back and shrug.

"I've known about this for a while, as have a few others, including the exec team, and we think we have a great addition to the team here. I want to introduce you to my replacement." He opens his arm in the direction of the blonde mystery woman. "This is Jaqueline Bellingham. She will be taking over for me as VP of IT. I think she will hit the ground running and be a wonderful new voice with great vision. Now, I'll let her introduce herself to all of you."

Bob steps forward and takes a seat in the front row as Jaqueline stands up and faces the department. She does not show one sign of nervousness. She is confident and sure. She speaks with authority, but also with kindness.

"Hello, everyone," she says. "It is great to meet you all. This is pretty formal, but I am going to take the opportunity to meet with you individually or in small groups to get to know you better. I am really thankful for this opportunity and for Bob and KPM giving me a chance to make a difference here. Not only am I an IT Champion, but I am also versed in Inclusion and Diversity. I was the I and D leader at my previous company, and I'd like to bring some of that knowledge here to

KPM. I will also be sending out a brief, anonymous, survey with a few questions I have. I'd like you to fill it out before I meet with all of you. I am sure you have lots of questions for me just as I have for you. I hope that you will all help me get up to speed with our department and with KPM, and I will help all of you as much as I can. I look forward to working with all of you. Thank you."

Jaqueline sits back down, and Bob returns to the front of the department.

"She seems nice," Nick whispers to me.

Yeah, she does. She seems genuinely nice. Plus, Inclusion and Diversity sounds perfect. If only I had the guts to talk to her about my anxiety.

Maybe she will have a one-on-one meeting with you.

Oh, God, no! I'd die.

But you just said…

I know, but I don't have the guts.

She seems so nice and to genuinely care. You'd be more likely to talk about it with just her than in a small group.

Yes, but I'm also more likely to freak out and puke.

"Okay," Bob says to quell the hushed whispers around the room. "I know this is a lot to take in right now. I will be here for any questions, as will Jaqueline. I'd also like to invite you all to my retirement party. It will be a week from Friday. You will all be receiving an Outlook invite with details. I hope that every one of you can make it. I've loved working here and with all of you."

Holy moly. This is actually happening.

You know you have to go to that party, right?

Shit.

CHAPTER TWO

I shoot a quick text to Brittany that says, "On my way," lean my head against the seat, and look out the car window. The green crossover pulls away from the curb in front of my building, and the driver doesn't seem to want to engage in conversation, which is perfectly fine by me. In fact, it is preferred.

It is Thursday evening. I am meeting Brittany at her apartment building so that Ed can pick us up and drive us to Foxwoods. The three of us are staying two nights and driving home on Saturday.

Why am I actually going to a management conference?

Gemma, give yourself some credit. Your boss thinks that you have management potential.

That doesn't even make sense.

Well, at least, you get a day off of work. And it's on a Friday, so it's kind of like you have a long weekend. And you will be in Foxwoods. It's actually a pretty good deal. So, you have to listen to some presentations about management. That's a small price to pay for a day off and a free stay at Foxwoods with your friend Brittany.

That is a good point. It's just a management conference. I don't actually have to do anything or manage anyone right now. I just have to sit and listen. I think I can handle that.

Well, you can handle the sitting part anyway.

As the car pulls to a stop, I can see Brittany standing on the sidewalk with a small rolling suitcase sitting on the ground next to her. Getting out of the car, I pull my own rolling suitcase off of the seat and drag it out onto the ground before closing the door.

"Hey!" Brittany says.

"Hey," I respond.

"I thought I'd just meet you out here. Ed has already texted that he is on his way."

"All right. This trip should be interesting."

"Oh, it will be fun. Just you wait and see."

I really hope she's right.

Ed pulls up in his car and pulls over to the curb.

"I call back seat," I say before Ed gets out of the car.

"What? No. You can't call back seat. You are only allowed to call shotgun."

"Not true. I called it. Back seat is mine."

"No fair."

"You're the talkative one. It only makes sense."

"He's going to talk the whole time."

"Yeah, but just let him talk. All you have to do is nod and smile. Maybe laugh once or twice."

"Fine," she says as she steps around to the back of the car where Ed is standing.

He motions to the open trunk. "Load 'em up," he says.

Brittany and I place our bags into the trunk and get into the car. It's a roomy sedan, silver, and not at all what I pictured Ed driving. I don't know what I pictured, but this wasn't it. This car is definitely a dad car. Which I guess is what he is.

"I hope you don't mind," he says as we pull away from the curb, "but I made a playlist for us. It's mostly 90's pop and R&B."

Oh, my God. Now that *is* what I expected.

The drive is about two hours from Boston to a Native American reservation in Connecticut. The casino is owned and operated by the Mashantucket Pequot Tribal Nation and has six casinos in the complex, as well as three hotels. We are staying in the hotel that is named the Fox Tower, which is, as I hear, a bit of a walk from most of the casinos and the other hotels.

"And that's when Lucy spilled the water all over the kitchen floor," Ed says.

"Lucy is your daughter?" Brittany asks.

"No, Danni is my daughter. Lucy is my cat."

"Oh, okay."

I glance at Brittany who is nodding her head. She slowly turns to look out her window, and I turn to look out mine.

Once out of Boston, the highway drive is mostly lined by trees and signs for exits and food and lodging. I let my eyes lose focus as the red, yellow, and brown leaves swish by as Aaliyah sings to the beat.

As we get closer, the towers of Foxwoods appear to rise from the horizon. They are beautiful, white, high-rise buildings with aqua-green roofs and aqua tinted windows up and down the sides of the buildings. The larger building is the main Foxwoods building, holding most of the casinos and guest rooms. The other building, the Fox Tower, is where we will be staying.

"It is about a half mile walk from inside the Fox Tower to the main Foxwoods casino building," Ed says.

"I guess we will be getting our exercise this weekend," Brittany answers.

"Well, there is a casino right outside the Fox Tower. So, in theory, we don't really have to leave the Fox Tower area."

"Where is the fun in that?" Brittany asks.

"Ah, exactly," Ed replies, and I can see him smile in the rearview mirror.

We turn into the compound. Roads and signs point and veer off in every direction. Our car drives up the garage self-park line and makes a turn into the third level. Ed parks the car, and we all grab our bags, walk through the garage to the elevators, and ride down to the casino floor. As we walk out of the elevator, the sounds of dinging, ringing, buzzing, and clinking surround us. The ugly patterned red and orange carpet leads us right into the casino. We follow the walkway around the slot machines and turn to the right, away from the chaos and into the hotel lobby.

The lobby is huge, and the ceiling has to be a hundred feet high. In the middle is a fountain with cushioned seats all around it. Out of the windows on the left, I can see the swimming pool.

I stand in line behind Ed and Brittany. We all check in together, get our keys, and head back in the direction of the casino.

"I can't believe we've all got our own rooms," Brittany says.

"I know," I respond. "It's really nice."

Walking in the walkway around the casino and to the right we find the entrance to the hotel elevators. Somehow, they managed to get us all rooms on the same floor.

"Okay, you guys," Ed says. "I don't know about you, but I'm starving."

"Me too!" Brittany responds.

"Same here," I say.

"Then how about we settle into our roomie-rooms, take a pee break, and regroup back together in twenty minutes?" Ed suggests.

"Ten minutes," Brittany counters.

"Woman after my own heart," Ed replies. "Ten minutes it is."

I roll my suitcase down the hall, stop in front of my assigned door, and swipe the key. The room is luxurious. A single king-sized bed is in the middle of it, and a large wooden bureau with a TV on top sits across from the bed. A small coffee table with a bench is right in front of the window, which provides a beautiful view of all the leaves changing colors.

What is it called, all of those trees?

A forest?

No. There's no pine trees. Is that still a forest?

Yes? Or is it woods?

Anyway, it's lovely.

Peeking into the bathroom, I see a beautiful porcelain counter that looks almost like marble, with a sink buried into it and a shower next to it.

What are you looking for? It's the instant coffeemaker, right? It's there on the counter.

Just in case.

Just in case? There are probably plenty of places to get coffee on the casino level that are far better than that coffee. You can probably even get free coffee if you are playing any of the games.

Like I said, just in case.

Anyway, just go pee and then go meet your coworkers.

Aye, aye.

I scamper down to the elevators where Brittany and Ed are already waiting for me.

"Where shall we go?" Brittany asks as we ride quickly down the elevator.

Man, that elevator really accelerates when there are no stops in between. I think I almost lost my stomach.

For once, I am slightly light headed due to something other than anxiety.

Shake it off.

"I vote for the Scorpion Bar," Ed responds.

"Never heard of it," Brittany replies.

"All the more reason to go," Ed says.

Brittany looks at me, and I shrug.

"Okay," she says. "Let's do it."

They turn to look at me.

I don't even know what kind of food it serves. Based on the limited information I have about the restaurant, it sounds like it serves chilled scorpions, maybe prepared like a shrimp cocktail.

How bad could it be?

Based on that information, pretty bad.

Just go with the flow, Gemma.

"Why not?" I add.

"Great! Follow me, ladies," Ed says as he exits the elevator with an excited hop.

Brittany hangs behind for a moment and stops beside me. "I'm sorry. I really didn't think Ed would want to hang out with us at all."

"It's okay. It's kind of nice to have someone that knows where he is going in this giant place."

Even if it is to eat scorpions.

Brittany smiles, and we speed up to catch Ed. We walk for what seem like a mile, up escalators, past restaurants and ice cream shops, by windows overlooking the trees, and into another area with shops and restaurants.

Looking down one of the pathways, I turn to see Brittany pull in behind Ed when he stops in front of a giant wooden door. I do the same. There are no windows looking into the restaurant.

"It looks ominous," Brittany notes.

Yes. We are definitely eating scorpions. Hopefully they are dead at the time.

"Yep, we're still going in, though," Ed replies.

I look at Brittany and grin. "After you," I say.

Ed pulls open the big wooden door to reveal a darkly lit restaurant with a large bar across the wall to the left and tables in the center of the room. There are booths along the walls and all the way at the back of the room, up some stairs. A waitress comes up to us.

"Sit wherever you'd like," she says and walks away.

"This is sexy," Ed says.

"What do you think those are supposed to be?" Brittany asks, pointing to what appear to be wooden sticks, with curves much like branches running up the walls and along the ceiling.

"Bones of their enemies," Ed says.

We wander to the back of the restaurant, up a couple of steps, and sit in a semi-circular booth, with Ed in the middle.

The same waitress brings over menus and asks, "Drinks to start? We have half price house margaritas until nine."

I glance down at the menu. It's a Mexican restaurant. I scan the appetizers. No scorpions. Thank God. Ed definitely would have made us get one.

"Margs?" Ed asks. "Oh, heck yes."

"For you?" the waitress asks Brittany and me.

"I'll have a margarita, too," Brittany replies.

Oh, why not?

"I will too," I say.

"That's my girl," Ed responds.

"This place is cool," Brittany says as the waitress steps away.

"The food is good, too," Ed replies.

"You've been here before?" I ask.

"Oh, yeah, baby."

"That's right. You have a car," Brittany says and laughs.

"That I do."

"Where do you park it for work?" I ask.

"Work? Oh, no. I don't drive to work." He laughs and says, "I couldn't handle rush hour. I take the train."

"The train?" Brittany and I ask at the same time.

"Yes. It's this magical tube that takes you places with a bunch of strangers."

"Huh," I say. "Never heard of such a thing."

"You should look into it. It's all the rage. How do you get to work, Brittany, if you've never heard of a train?"

Brittany rolls her eyes. "I take the T."

"Ah, yes," Ed says. "The mini magic tube."

"I was just surprised that you didn't drive, that is all," Brittany responds.

"I just didn't know what a train was," I say.

"Yes, well, you do live close to work," Ed replies.

The waitress returns with three margaritas and places one down in front of each of us.

"Do you know what you'd like to order?" she asks.

Crap, I didn't even look at the menu. I just ruled out predatory arachnids.

Make that all arachnids.

"I will have the cheeseburger burrito," Brittany says.

"Hey, that's what I'm getting!" Ed shouts.

All three turn to look at me.

Actually, that sounds really good.

"Oh, fine. I'll get it, too."

"Triplets!" Ed yells as the waitress walks away as fast as she can. "You guys are the best."

"We know," Brittany replies.

"So," Ed inquires, "are you going to hit up the casino after this, ladies?"

"I am in," Brittany responds.

They turn to look at me.

Am I in? No. It will be too late. We have a conference in the morning. We have to get up early.

Gemma, seriously? It is just a conference, one that you don't even want to go to. Plus, you are at Foxwoods for the very first time. For free. Live a little, would you?

"I'm in."

"Yes!" Brittany and Ed shout at the same time.

"What games do you guys play?" I ask.

"I like to play Black Jack," Ed answers. "Sometimes Craps if I am feeling lucky." He smiles.

There's no way I can play either of those.

"Don't worry," Brittany says. "I only play the slot machines. You can stick with me."

"Do you guys know who else is coming from KPM to the conference?" I ask.

"They told me," Ed replies, "but I don't remember. Should we reach out to them?"

Brittany and I look at each other, scrunch our faces, and look back at Ed.

"Yeah, I don't know why I even asked that. Gross."

The waitress returns with our burritos and quickly leaves before any of us can speak to her.

Ed looks down at his plate and yells, "Delish!"

"Oh my God, I'm in heaven," Brittany says and takes a second bite.

All right, girl. Let's try this. You are living life this weekend.

I take a bite.

"Oh, my God, it has French fries in it!" I involuntarily shout.

Ed and Brittany grin at me.

"Good right?" Brittany asks.

"For sure."

There is not much conversation as we all devour our burritos. When the waitress returns to check on us, we order another round of margaritas.

"I have to say," Ed says. "I was a little worried about coming here with coworkers, but this is all right."

Brittany and I look at each other and then answer at the same time, "I agree."

"As long as we don't run into anyone else from KPM."

"Oh, God, yes," Brittany and I again say at the same time.

"You two are cute," Ed says and smiles.

"We know," Brittany replies.

As we finish eating, the waitress brings us the bill.

Oh, right the bill.

"I talked Andy into giving me his company card," Ed says as he flashes it up from the table.

"What!" Brittany shouts.

"Why are you so awesome?" I ask.

"Baby, I was born this way," Ed says.

I giggle as the waitress takes the card and immediately returns.

Damn, she really wants us to leave, huh?

"All right," Brittany says as we push open the large wooden door and reenter the bustling Foxwoods corridors. "Where to?"

"The Grand Cedar Casino is closest," Ed says.

I shrug. "Sounds good to me."

We walk past the sign that tells us we have to be twenty-one years or older to enter, and my feet once again shuffle on a hideous orange and red carpet.

"I'm off to the tables!" Ed waves as he leaves us behind.

"That wasn't so bad," Brittany says.

"It was actually pretty fun."

"And see, Ed won't be spending the whole time with us. He likes to gamble at the tables."

"I will never be that cool."

"Yes, we all strive to be as cool as Ed."

I follow Brittany around as she scopes out the slot machines, looking at the game and how much each costs. We find two slots next to each other and sit down. Each spin is a cent; however, slot machines, Brittany explains, never let you bet just one penny. Each spin is at least twenty-five cents, if not more.

So, freaking rude. Why say it's a penny if that is not even an option? False advertising, I say.

That's how they get you.

That's how they get my money.

The seat is plastic, but not uncomfortable, with a cushioned back. It is bolted to the floor, but swivels.

Lots of chair thieves around?

I look at the loud, musical, and colorful screen in front of me. The screen simulates a game, which takes less than a second before it reads, "game over." Animated bunnies and carrots roll around the screen and then stop. Seemingly unrelated lines crisscross over the screen.

"How does this work?" I ask.

"You just put your money in like this," she responds as her twenty-dollar bill is sucked into the machine. "You can see your balance right here," she says and points to the bottom right corner of the screen. "And then, you push this button until all of your money disappears."

I laugh. "Brittany, the point is to try to win, right?"

"Yeah, but there's no real strategy. You are just at the mercy of the machine."

That would make a good name for a band.

"What about these options?" I ask, pointing to the different buttons in front of me.

"That's how quickly you want your money to disappear."

"You mean, they are different amounts to bet?"

"Yeah, that's what I said."

I smile. "Okay. I get it. How do I know if I win?"

"You won't. The lines are crazy weird. The machine will tell you."

I nod. "Sounds fun."

"Ladies!" Ed walks up behind us. "Did you know that if you are gambling, the drinks are free?"

Say, what?

"Happy hunting!" he says and disappears behind a line of slot machines.

All right. Let's line 'em up.

"Did he just reappear to tell us that?" I ask.

"Knowing him, probably."

Good, man.

Quickly losing our first twenty dollars, we get up and search for two more machines next to each other. We wander around the casino and then out into the corridor and into another casino and do the same thing multiple times until my stack of bills gets smaller and smaller. Brittany and I then wander through the long and bustling pathways people watching and looking into store windows.

"I feel like we've been walking for miles," I say.

"I think that's because we have," Brittany replies.

"Let's sit down on this bench for a minute."

In front of us is a giant fake rock formation with a statue of a Native American, made of an opaque glass, kneeling down and shooting a bow and arrow into the sky. Above him is a ceiling made of windows, so we can see the sky. This must be really pretty during the day.

"Oh, my feet," Brittany says as she sits down on the bench in front of the rock formation.

"I didn't realize how huge this place is. We must be four miles from our hotel rooms."

"Normally, I would think that's an exaggeration, but I actually think that's pretty accurate."

I lean back against the bench and stretch my legs out straight in front of me.

"I wonder what Ed is doing," I say.

"Probably wandering around with a drink in his hand and just being Ed."

"Making friends with everyone he sees."

How nice must that be? To make friends with anyone you meet and not be afraid to speak to them.

"Oh!" Brittany yells.

I sit up straight and look at her.

"We need to send Nick a selfie."

"Why?"

"To rub it in his face that he's not here and to show him how much fun we're having."

"Oh, of course."

"Should we do it now?"

"No time like the present."

She reaches into her purse, pulls out her phone, and holds it in front of us.

"No wait!" she says. "Let's walk out a bit so we can get the statue behind us in the picture."

I agree, and we proceed to take a picture, scrutinize it, delete it, and then take another until we are satisfied. Well, maybe not satisfied, but have concluded that it is the best it's going to get.

"You know," I say. "The statue of the Native American looks better than we do."

"You're right. Look at him. He's glowing."

Literally. He is glowing. A light is illuminating him.

"Oh, well. Nick won't care," I say.

"No. Let's put a filter on the picture. Make us look better."

"For Nick? He really won't care."

"Okay there. That's better, right?"

"Mmm. Statue still looks better than I do."

Brittany grins and hits send. Nick responds immediately. "I am so jealous! Looks like you guys are having so much fun!"

I wouldn't say that picture conveys that much fun. But, okay.

Brittany types out a message, reads his response, and then types out another while smiling to herself.

Hmmm. Look at this development.

"Uh, I think we should start walking back before the sun goes down and the coyotes come out," I say.

No response. She's still reading texts from Nick.

"Brit? You want to start walking back before the vampires come out?"

"Huh?"

"Want to start our long sojourn back to Fox Tower?"

"Oh, yes! Do you want to hit up some casinos on the way back? Maybe get some more drinks?"

"Of course. I still have some cash I can lose."

Not much, Gemma. Remember you are staying tomorrow night too. You need some cash for...life.

I have my ATM card. I will be fine.

Look at you going with the flow! Even if it is to the detriment of your bank account.

Shush.

As we walk back, our steps get slower and slower. We stop at the first casino, look at each other, shake our heads and keep walking. At the next casino, we stop, and I sigh.

"I'm too tired," Brittany says.

"Oh, thank goodness. I am too."

"Okay, let's just hike back to our rooms then?"

"Great plan. I just wish I brought a hiking stick."

Once back in the hotel, I open the door, flip off my shoes, and place my purse onto the bureau. Pulling out my phone, I hit the video call button and wait while it connects.

"Hey, you."

McGruff's beautiful face appears on my phone.

"Hey, yourself," I say.

His eyes light up. "Are you drunk?"

What? Of course, I am. It's pretty obvious.

"No."

He smiles. "I must be mistaken."

"Yep," I respond as I flop down onto the bed and roll onto my back with the phone above my face.

"How's the hotel?" he asks.

"It's so nice. We each have our own room, and I have a great view of all the fall foliage. It's like a forest of trees…with leaves. You know, not pine trees."

He laughs. "Yeah, I understand. What have you been doing there?"

"Well, Brittany and Ed and I went to dinner. Don't get mad. Ed is married."

McGruff frowns. "We've been over this. I'm not jealous of any of your coworkers. Okay?"

"Okay. So, we went to the Scorpion Bar for dinner. It's so cool. And dark. I had a burrito with French fries in it. And we played slot machines. Did you know that they give you free drinks if you are

34

gambling? Because they do. They just walk around handing out free drinks to people. Why are you smiling?"

"You're a lot more talkative when you're drunk."

"So I've been told."

His eyes twinkle at me.

"What are your plans for tomorrow?"

"Just stupid conference stuff. Probably some more slot machines. They do have a lot of outlet stores that I may wander through. I don't know. I'm sure Brittany and Ed have their own thoughts about it."

"I'm sure they do."

"How are you? What is up with you?"

"Oh, not much. Just some…"

I roll over onto my side and tuck the pillow up underneath my cheek. My eyes start to close.

"Are you listening to me?" McGruff asks.

What? No.

"Yes," I mumble.

What is he saying then?

"How much did you have to drink? You know you aren't supposed to drink a lot while taking your anxiety medication."

"I know. I didn't."

"Okay, good. So, I was saying…"

My eyes can't focus. He looks fuzzy on my phone. Is that the phone or my vision?

Probably your vision. You are very drunk. Are you even listening to him? Look. He looks like he's saying things. They could be important things. Maybe listen.

But I don't.

Your eyes are closing, Gemma. Stay awake.

"Gemma?"

"Hmm?"

"I'll let you sleep."

Gem of Resiliency

Say goodbye, Gemma.

But I don't.

My eyes close, and the phone drops from my hand.

CHAPTER THREE

I am again standing in line behind Ed and Brittany, this time in the meeting center near the Fox Tower. As the line slowly creeps forward, I glance around at the other people dressed in business casual attire going to this management conference. Ed is handed a packet and a couple pieces of paper by the man sitting at the table in front of the line. Ed slaps on a nametag and turns to look at Brittany and then to me with a strange twinkle in his eye. He walks a couple of paces to his left and stands to wait for us.

I don't know what that look was about, but I do not like it.

It could be nothing.

That was not nothing.

Brittany reaches out and accepts the same folder and pieces of paper. She puts on her nametag and then turns to give me a twinkle-eyed look.

I do not like this one bit. What is happening up there? Are they brainwashing people? Why are they looking at me like that?

Well, you're about to find out. Step up.

I step forward as the man behind the table looks up at me.

"Name and company?" he asks.

"Gemma Green with KPM Insurance."

"Gemma Green, GG," he replies as he searches for my name.

Nope. Don't like that at all.

"All right," he says, "With KPM. Here is your nametag. We ask that you wear it so that it can be readily seen. Here is your packet with the schedule of presentations and some welcome information. And everyone at the conference gets a free ticket to both the car races and the zipline. Have a great day."

And there it is. They are going to make me screech down the zipline at full speed. Yes, they are.

Don't forget the car races. They are definitely going to make you race around the track, as well.

Damn it, Joe. Why'd you have to bail last minute on this conference? Here I am on some sort of management track at work and have a mini project to lead, and, oh, I also have to go ziplining now, too.

You don't have to go.

Did you see how they looked at me? They are definitely making me go.

Why do you let people make you do things you don't want to? You can say no.

I walk over to where the two of them have been waiting and put on my nametag.

"Looks like our first presentation is right over there," I say and point over to the left.

"Then, we'll have enough time before the second one to go ziplining," Ed says.

"I don't think I'm going to do that," I say.

Look at you saying no!

"Really?" Brittany asks. "How often do you get the chance to do it? And it's free."

Damn it. She is right.

Wait. No. You were just so happy that you actually said no to something. You can't take it back now.

Yes. I can. I can change my mind. I am going with the flow, remember?

"So?" Ed asks.

Yeah, so?

"I'll think about it," I answer.

Brittany smiles. "That's not a no."

"Booya!" Ed exclaims.

Why are you even considering ziplining?

38

Why not, honestly?

You've got me there. Why not?

I trail after Ed and Brittany as we follow the crowd into a room with lines of chairs facing a giant screen that says, "Management."

"Well, this looks all sorts of fun," Ed says as he shuffles down a row of chairs and sits.

Brittany and I follow and sit with him. We are in the middle of the row and in the middle of the room. People are all around us.

Great, this is a breeding ground for anxiety.

Just breathe. You don't know any of these people. You will never see any of them again. You don't have to feel weird.

I *know* I don't. But that doesn't mean I won't.

At least, you aren't sitting in the front row.

A man, probably in his fifties, with grey hair and a grey mustache and holding a clicker for the computer screen behind him, walks in front of the crowd.

"Welcome, everyone, to our first presentation on management this morning."

I look over at Ed, who brings his hand up to his mouth and fakes a yawn.

How am I at a management conference?

Damn it, Gemma. You are. Get over it.

I furrow my brow at my own thoughts.

Geez, Louise. I was just pondering why on this green earth Carl would think I could be management.

Pay attention! You are here for a reason.

What is that reason, again? I have yet to figure it out.

Because you are on the management track at work. Now, pay attention.

I reluctantly listen as this stranger tells us how to succeed at being a manager and managing people.

"Take command of the meeting," he says.

Never have I ever.

"Delegate work."

I'd rather do it myself. It will get done correctly.

"Be clear about expectations, set deadlines, and follow up to make sure deadlines are met."

I pass.

"Always communicate effectively."

No. I don't even effectively communicate with myself.

"Go to bat for your employees."

I don't think I can do that.

"Listen."

Oh! One I might be able to do.

Can you?

Yes...

Yes, you can listen as long as you aren't exceedingly anxious or thinking about something else, which is most of the time.

When I am a manager, I will always be exceedingly anxious and thinking about other things, so I can do none of these bullet points that make a good manager. Great. I am glad I got roped into coming to this conference just so I can feel like shit about my management potential.

Girl, you already felt like that. Chin up.

"Ready?"

My head snaps to the right to see Ed and Brittany staring at me as the meeting room empties.

Yeah, why not jump off the roof. Seems like a fitting activity at this point.

Gemma!

"Yep, let's go," I respond.

Following the mass exodus from the conference room, we take an elevator up to the zipline landing zone.

Why am I so nervous?

Because you are literally jumping off the roof of a building.

Oh right.

The elevator doors open, and my stomach drops. I must say, a lot of my time is spent quelling anxiety nausea, but this nausea is worse. The few people in front of us are already heading out onto the roof, so we step right up to the font.

Just breathe. Now is no time to faint.

Out there on the roof is no time to faint either.

Fair point. If you're going to faint, do it now.

"We will go at the same time, okay?" Brittany says to me as the employees fasten us into our harnesses.

Okay? Why did I agree to this?

Because you wanted to have fun. You can still say no and go back down the way you came up, in the elevator not off the roof.

No, I should do this. How many times will I get the opportunity to go ziplining like this?

And for free.

Exactly. So why do I feel like I should have worn an adult diaper?

It will be fine. I'm sure no one has died on it.

Died! I wasn't even thinking about dying.

"Does that feel tight enough?" the guy manhandling me asks.

Does it? I bloody well hope so. I want to be suffocating in it for crying out loud.

"Yes?"

"It'll be okay," he says as he yanks one more time on the straps wrapped around my body.

We are standing just inside the doors on metal ramps that lead out to the roof. My hands are shaking as I see Ed practically prance on his way out to the roof.

Just breathe.

How did I get myself into this mess?

By going with the flow.

Damn the flow!

Following Brittany out the doors, I feel the cool autumn breeze wash over me. The cheers of the couple going out now slowly dissipate as they get farther away. As I walk out onto the roof, the cool autumn air turns into a whipping, cold wind.

I think I'm going to be sick.

No, you're not. Just breathe.

I can feel my heartbeat speed up and my breathing become shallow. My hands start to shake.

No! This is fine. You are fine. You've had to speak one on one with the vice president. This is nothing.

True. I'd much rather be ziplining than having a meeting with the CEO.

Oh, God, don't jinx yourself.

"I'll go first," Ed shouts into the wind.

He steps forward to the two zipline employees waiting for him. They help him up a couple of steps and hook his harness to the apparatus above him. When he is fully attached, the harness basically acts as a floating chair. At least, I don't actually have to hold on to something to keep myself on the line. The chair will just go and take me with it. Why did I think that I'd have to hold on to some sort of bar across the zipline like a burglar would in a movie scene?

Gemma, there is no way a company would let you do that. There's too much liability.

Well, thank God!

Watching Ed dangling above the Fox Tower roof, ready for his adventure, I then turn to look out over the tree tops, the same tree tops that form the pine-tree-less forest outside my hotel window. Despite being scared, I am captivated by the beautiful sight.

"You okay?" Brittany leans in and asks me.

Who? Me? I'm the pinnacle of calm.

"Yep. I think I can do this without pooping my pants. Peeing is another story."

"Gemma, we'll be fine."

"Ready?" the man asks Ed, who is kicking his feet in the air in anticipation.

"Absolutely!" he responds. "Ladies!" Ed yells over his shoulder to us. "I will see you down there!"

He turns back to look out over the zipline course and waits for the employee to unhitch him to begin his descent down from the roof. As he starts to roll down the line, Ed shouts, "Party on!" with his fist in the air. "Yahoooooooo!"

I can hear his voice get farther and farther away. His body gets smaller and smaller until I can no longer see it.

That really looks like fun. I mean, if I didn't have a giant knot in my stomach, and I wasn't absolutely certain I'd be vomiting the whole way down.

"You ready?" Brittany asks.

"Yep. Let's get into our contraptions."

My heart is beating faster and faster as I step up the couple of stairs in front of me to the hanging cord that will keep me from plunging to my death.

Do not pass out. Do not pass out.

Do not barf. Do not barf.

"I can't believe we are doing this!" Brittany shouts as we are loaded into our belts and gizmos.

The set up makes it so we are sitting in this hanging seat of ropes and straps.

"Ready?" the man at the front of the line asks us.

"Ready!" Brittany responds immediately.

They both look at me.

"Ready..."

Here we go!

I look down at my feet hanging from the cradle of the harness, only the open air in front of me. I can hear the man behind me unhitch me from the roof.

I take a huge breath. Let's do this.

43

"Party on!" I yell as I roll off of the rooftop and out into the air over the treetops.

The main building of the Foxwoods resort is to our left, the green around the windows is shimmering in the sunlight. My heartbeat begins to slow as I descend down the wire, the wind pushing tears out of the sides of my eyes.

It's a bit chilly up here, probably should have worn a coat.

"You okay over there?" I hear Brittany yell from my right.

Twisting my head in her direction, I see her gracefully floating through the air.

"Yeah!" is all I can muster to yell back.

The autumn colored trees rush swiftly by, just below my feet, and as I get closer to the ground, they are barely out of reach. I close my eyes as the wind rushes by my face. I feel like a bird.

Spread your wings.

What?

Put out your arms.

What? No. I can't let go.

Why not? You're not going to fall out.

I start by quickly jutting my fingers out off of the cord. Next, I remove one hand and instantly replace it.

Okay, I can do this. Rip off the band-aid. All at once. One. Two. Three.

I breathe in and spread my arms out to each side. My head tips back in the wind, and my chest lets out a huge breath. I can feel a smile spread across my face.

I am a bird.

The wind picks up and jostles me to the side. I immediately draw my arms back in and clutch the cord.

I was a bird.

Yes, you were.

Oh, geez. How does this end? Do I just bail and land on the dirt?

Goodness, Gemma, no.

Are you sure?

Well, no.

The ground gets closer and the tree tops are replaced with dirt and grass. I can see people waiting for us. When we get closer, the zipline swings to a halt, and two guys run up to me.

"How was it?" one asks as he drags me over to another set of steps.

"Fun," I instinctively say.

Taking my hands from the rope holding my harness to the zipline, I suddenly realize how tight I had been holding. There are indentations in both of my palms.

The guys unhook my harness and help me out of it.

"Would you do it again?" the other asks me.

"Yes!" I reply.

"Yeah!" one of the guys says. "That's what we like to hear."

Was that a lie?

No.

I wobble down the two steps as Brittany walks over to me.

"Was that fun or what?"

That was definitely fun.

"That was fun!" I reply as we make our way to Ed, who is waiting for our landing.

"Yeah!" Ed shouts and punches the air in front of him a few times. Once we give the thumbs up, he gives us both a high five.

I hear the next batch of zipliners screeching to a halt behind us.

"Let's go straight to the race cars," Ed suggests. "This was too much fun."

Wait, what? I barely have had any time to breathe. In fact, I am not sure I have yet.

"Why not? Let's go!" Brittany answers.

They both turn to look at me.

"Won't we be late for the next presentation?"

Yes, we will. We definitely will.

My chest tightens and feels like my heart has stopped.

Ed and Brittany glance at each other.

"Maybe. Maybe not," Ed responds.

Oh, we absolutely will be late. Why do they want to go right now?

"It's okay. We don't have to go now," Brittany says.

But I can tell she wants to. And I know Ed definitely wants to.

Oh, Gemma. It's okay. Do it. Live a little. Go with the flow? You don't always have to be so perfect.

No, I don't. I don't have to be perfect. It's okay to not be perfect. I'm not sure this is what Stacey meant when she originally told me that self-talk phrase, but this is how I am using it now. It's okay to not be perfect. It's okay to not be perfect!

That's it! Go girl!

"Oh, all right. Let's go now," I say.

"Really?" Brittany asks.

"Really."

"Yes! Let's go!" Ed shouts.

A broad smile stretches across my face.

After a trek back to Fox Tower and down into the parking garage, we arrive at the race track.

We are definitely going to be late for the next presentation.

Oh, shush!

The squealing and shrieking of tires are all I can hear as we wait in line to get our helmets and our cars. The cars look exactly like race cars, only smaller, but obviously, they are not real cars.

This race track doesn't look as terrifying as the zipline. I think I can drive one of these cars.

Yes, you absolutely can. You get eight minutes to whip around the track.

Brittany is practically bouncing up and down with excitement next to me.

"This looks like so much fun!" she yells.

"I am going to smoke you guys!" Ed shouts.

My heart is beating with, wait, what is that? With excitement. My heart is beating with excitement! I am practically bouncing up and down with excitement just like Brittany.

The next three cars are ours. Each of us puts on our respective helmet and climbs into the waiting car. An employee walks by to make sure we are adequately strapped in and then signals for Ed, then Brittany, and then for me to cut loose.

And away I go!

With the steering wheel in my hands and the track laid out in front of me, it feels like a video game, but centrifugal force and the wind in my face are real. The car skids a few times as I get a handle on the curves of the track, but after that I am buzzing down the course with the wind in my hair with no worries in my mind.

Pure joy. That is the only way I can describe it. I feel like a kid again.

My car squeals and screeches around the track as my mouth breaks out into a huge smile.

If only this feeling could last forever.

Racing around the track, I wave at Brittany and Ed whenever I see them. As I get more comfortable, I speed up and cut the corners as close as I can. The wheels on my car screech and skid with every turn as I rev the engine and speed up. Toot toot! I honk the horn as I fly by Ed going the opposite direction. Brittany does the same when she passes by.

When the eight minutes run out, and my car screams to a halt, I laugh uncontrollably. Taking my helmet off, I keep laughing, belly laughs, head thrown back in delight laughter.

I had so much fun.

The smile on my face does not disappear as I unstrap and exit my vehicle.

"Yeah!" Ed yells. "Score one for team KPM! Excellent!"

Excellent, indeed. I don't remember the last time I had that much fun. I don't even care that we have to sneak into the back of the conference room in the middle of the next presentation. The smile has not left my face.

CHAPTER FOUR

With drink in hand, I hit the button and watch the flashing reels roll on the screen. Glancing to my right, I watch Brittany as she does the same. Out of the corner of my eye, I see Ed pass by our row of slot machines and then back up and walk over to us.

"Guys, don't fall in love with me, but I got us tickets to The Shrine tonight," he says.

"The Shrine?" I ask.

"Yeah. It's a night club. There's a DJ tonight. Hope you brought your party shoes."

Why does it not surprise me that Ed wants to go dancing tonight? That definitely fits with how I was expecting this night to go.

"I'm in if Gemma's in," Brittany replies.

They both slowly turn their heads towards me and raise their eyebrows.

So? Are you in? Are you in to go dancing with two coworkers? Something you swore you'd never do.

That was dancing at a work party, this is different. Besides, it might be fun.

Fun? Who are you right now? Are you drunk?

Well, yes.

"I'm in!"

Did you really just say that?

"Yes!" Brittany shouts and claps her hands.

Ed raises his right arm, his fist in the air. "Party on! This is going to be killer! All right, let's go regroup, put on our clubbing attire, and meet back here. Say in an hour?"

Clubbing attire? That's not in my vocabulary.

"Sounds good," Brittany answers for us.

"Great!" Ed shouts, skips towards the elevators, and disappears inside.

Brittany looks at me. "You good with this?"

"I mean, it's definitely past my bedtime, but since we're here…"

"That's my girl!"

"I didn't bring clubbing attire, though. Honestly, it never crossed my mind. But it should have, knowing that Ed was going to be with us."

"I did bring an outfit."

Of course, she did. She's so much cooler than I am.

"You know what we can do?" she continues. "We can go to the outlets and get an outfit for you." Her eyes twinkle a little.

I'm not hating this idea, and I am struggling to come up with an excuse not to do it. Does that mean I want to do it? Is this what other people feel? Is this what it feels like to want to do something? Am I smiling?

"Let's do it," I say.

"Yes!" Brittany mimics Ed and extends her arm and thrusts her fist into the air.

"Party on," I reply.

"We'll get you some shoes, too."

I look down at my sensible boots.

"They're fine," Brittany says. "They just aren't clubbing shoes."

Yes, why did I not think to bring clubbing shoes?

That thought has never crossed your mind.

"Okay, want to cash out or just let this ride?" Brittany asks me.

I look at the dollars on my screen; they are depressingly low.

"Let's let it ride. I only have a few more spins left on this machine anyway."

"Yeah, same here."

Hitting the button a few more times, I watch as my money disappears from the lower right hand corner of the screen.

"Well, that was easy," I say.

"All right! Let's get you some clothes."

Why is she more excited than I am?

The outlets at Foxwoods run from the Fox Tower all the way to the main Foxwoods building. We just have to walk out of the casino and up an escalator, and it's like we've been transported to a shopping mall. There are stores as far as the eye can see, with benches and plants in the middle of the corridor.

"This is amazing," I say. "How can this be the same place?"

"I know, right. Foxwoods has it all."

There is no hint of the casinos and buzzing and dinging of machines, just the marble floors and walls of what appears to be a stand-alone mall. I would believe I were in one, if I hadn't just left the casino.

We walk past a few stores before Brittany says, "This one," and veers to the right through the store's doors.

She peruses the tables and hangers and finds a shirt, holds it against my chest, and says, "Perfect."

"Do I get to keep my own jeans?" I ask.

She laughs. "Yes, those will do. Now for shoes."

I follow her to the back of the store where a few pairs are displayed on a table.

"Hmm, I guess these. I don't really want to go to another store, but we can if you don't like these," she says and looks at me.

"They're fine."

"Not the response I was hoping for, but okay. Do you want to try them on?"

"Probably should."

Brittany drops the shoes onto the ground, and I squish my feet into them.

"So?" she asks.

"They'll do."

"Again, not the response I was looking for, but okay. We don't have much time before we need to meet Ed."

We check out, hurry back down the escalators, through the casino, and back to our hotel rooms.

It's okay, Gemma. You actually look pretty good in this outfit. It's only one night. No one will see you dance.

There are plenty of people here.

No one you know will see you.

Hurriedly applying makeup, I check my texts to find that both Brittany and Ed are already making their way out of the hotel.

Shit.

Know what? Who cares what I look like? I don't know any of these people.

That's the spirit!

Ed and Brittany are just meeting up as I exit the elevator.

"Ladies! You both look smoking!" he shouts.

Yep. He is extremely drunk.

No, this is good. Maybe tomorrow he won't remember you dancing. Besides, you are pretty drunk yourself. Maybe you won't remember you dancing, either.

As long as there's no photographic evidence, I think it'll be fine.

"Let's go!" Brittany shouts and claps her hands once.

As we get close, I look up at the large shining sign that reads, "Shrine." There is what appears to be an Asian symbol above the door and two white statues on either side of the door. Following my coworkers inside, I am struck by the size of the place.

Yep. There is a disco ball.

The club is bathed in red light. In the back, there is a stage with the word "Shrine" hanging from a banner behind it. The DJ is looking out over the crowd that has gathered in front of him on the dance floor. They are dancing without a care and with their hands in the air.

That's going to be you soon. Look at Brittany and Ed. Look at how excited they are. You are going to be in that crowd dancing.

"I need a drink," I preemptively say.

Brittany nods and all three of us walk over to the square shaped bar in the center of the room. We have to push through the crowd and up to the bar only to wait for the bartender to notice us.

This would never happen at Flannery's.

No. Because there's never this many people there. Can you imagine how stressed Greg would be?

I can, and it's hilarious. He is used to tending the bar at Flannery's where he can take a few minutes to throw some darts. He would lose his mind with all these people wanting drinks.

Finally, we are served, and I clutch my glass as if I'm afraid it will jump away from me if held too loosely. My breath quickens each time I bring the straw up to my mouth to sip.

Calm down. The booze will do its job soon enough. Just wait it out. Take another sip.

"You two ready to go out onto the dance floor?" Ed asks.

Ready? No. I'm not nearly drunk enough.

"Five minutes," Brittany replies.

"All right. See you out there!" Ed says as he sashays away and disappears into the swarm on the dance floor.

I need more than five minutes.

You need more than five drinks.

Brittany pulls me over to her and leans in close.

"I have a drunken confession to make."

"Go on."

She brings her hand up to her ear and nervously traces her index finger around the lobe. Her eyes look into mine and then immediately dart to the right and stare into the crowd.

Should I prod her a little or just leave her be? She'll tell me if she wants to, right?

And if she doesn't want to?

I will live forever with the unanswered question of her Foxwoods drunken confession.

She leans in even closer and whispers into my ear, "I have a thing for Nick."

Instinctively, I step back and yell, "I knew it! I knew it! I knew it!"

"Okay! Okay! You don't have to be so happy."

"Why not? This is awesome."

"No, it's not."

"Why?"

"Because he has a thing for you."

"No, he doesn't. Not anymore. Not since I stomped on his little heart and chose McGruff."

Brittany smiles. "Still. He's probably not over you."

"No. I'm sure he is. It's been months and frankly, I'm not that great."

"Shut up! Yes, you are."

"Not as great as you. I always thought you two would be good together."

"I don't think he thinks that, though."

"You never know."

"He asked me to go with him to Bob's retirement party next Friday."

"Oh! You're his date!"

"No, it's not like that. We are going as friends. He knew you were taking Nate, so he wanted someone to talk to since he said you guys usually hang out at IT department meetings." She looks down to the floor and runs her hand through her hair. "Anyway, it's time to go dance with Ed."

Is it, though?

"Are you sure we have to do that?" I ask.

"Yes! It will be fun. I promise."

Will it be fun, though?

There's a 50/50 chance.

"Come on, Gem!" she pleads.

"I just need one more drink. I will meet you out there."

"You promise?"

Can I cross my fingers? That still absolves me of any lying I do, right?

Not since elementary school.

I sigh and roll my eyes. "Yes," I mutter.

"What was that? I couldn't hear you," she teases.

"I said yes!" I shout.

Brittany claps her hands. "Yes! We got you. Be out there soon, or I'll come find you."

And I know she will, too. She will definitely come find me.

Seriously, Gemma, are you really going to stand here alone all night? Go out and dance.

What? Wait. What?

Why not? Give me one good reason.

Because...dancing.

That is not a good reason.

I catch the bartender's eye, and he places another glass in front of me.

Look, you have your liquid courage. Go out and dance like you promised you would.

I can feel the beat of the music reverberating through my chest. The alcohol coursing through my veins has released the tension in my body. My heartbeat is smooth, my hands no longer shake, and my head begins to move to the beat.

Look at you loosening up.

Yeah, only took three drinks.

Maybe you should slow down, Gemma.

It's too late now.

Too late for what?

I'm going to dance.

Wait. What?

Yep. I'm going to shake my booty out on the floor and dance with Brittany and Ed.

Are you sure about this?

Yes. There is no one here that I know. Brittany and Ed are already dancing. They can't tell everyone at work about me dancing without me being able to do the same to them.

But...

I'm going.

Already moving to the music, I am now dancing as I make my way out to Brittany and Ed.

Raising her arms in the air, Brittany shouts, "Yes!" as she sees me.

"Yeah! Gemma!" Ed yells. "About time!"

The three of us form a circle, or rather a triangle, and dance like no one is watching. Because no one is. All these people are doing the same themselves. I've never felt so invisible and free and so sure that absolutely no one was watching me or caring what I was doing.

This is an amazing feeling. Is this what normal people feel like every day? They don't care what people think of them or if anyone is watching them? They just live? They just live without a care? It is so freeing.

I am suddenly aware that I am bouncing up and down with my hands in the air screaming whatever song is on at the top of my lungs as Brittany and Ed do the same.

Shit. I am having so much fun. Who would have thought that a work trip with Ed would make me so relaxed and that I could stand in a circle with Ed and Brittany jumping up and down, yelling lyrics at them, and pointing up to the ceiling?

I am free. I am a bird. I am lost in this moment of pure joy.

I close my eyes and breathe in, not because I have to regain my composure, but because I want to soak in the moment. Here I am, in the middle of the dance floor, with strangers bumping against me, and I am free. Jumping up and down, I am free.

"I need to tell you guys something," Ed yells as we all keep dancing. "I'm quitting my job!" he gleefully squeals, reaching his arms up to the sky.

"What? No! You can't!" Brittany yells back.

Ed laughs uncontrollably. "No! I'm not! But Larry is! He hasn't given his notice yet, so you are both sworn to secrecy."

Honestly, I probably won't remember this conversation, anyway.

"And you, Gemma!" He points at me, his arm stretched in my direction, his hips swaying back and forth. "I think you should replace him."

Brittany howls. "I think that's a great idea!"

"I know you'll mull it over," Ed says as he turns around and shakes his bottom at us.

"Ed!" I screech.

He laughs as he turns back around. "This is the best work trip I've ever been on!"

"Me too!" Brittany yells.

Me too.

"But you should apply for Larry's job, Gemma!" Ed yells again.

"Yes! You should," Brittany shouts at me.

I should? Should I?

The lights are beating down on my head, sweat is pouring down my face, and my head gets dizzy. I stop moving and put my hand to my head.

"Are you okay?" Brittany stops dancing and asks me.

"I just got really dizzy."

"Do you want me to get you some water?" Ed asks.

"No. No. I'm just going to go back to my room and lie down."

"Do you want me to come with you?" Brittany asks.

"No. I'll be fine. You both stay and have fun."

"Okay. Be safe," Brittany replies.

"Safe travels, Gemma," Ed says.

Taking one last look at the two of them bouncing up and down, my stomach lurches as I turn to push my way through the crowd.

See. You shouldn't have had so much to drink. Look at you. You can barely walk.

I know. It was dumb.

Yes. It was. You know you shouldn't even be drinking while you are taking Celexa, never mind so much.

Yeah. I know. But I needed to relax. And I'm glad I did. I had so much fun tonight.

Just remember that when you wake up hungover in the morning.

It was worth it for that moment of freedom and joy.

Finally making it to the hotel elevators, I wobble into the box with three other people, taking extra care to step over the slit of death, and I hit the button for my floor. Stepping backward until I hit the wall, I lean my head back against it.

"Rough night?" one of the elevator patrons asks me.

"Actually, it was most splendid."

"You win big?"

"No. I was free."

I may just be drunk, but the man looks confused and turns to face the front door again.

One of the other elevator riders looks at me, "This is you," she says.

I look at the open elevator doors and out into the hotel floor.

"Thank you," I slur as I stumble out of the box as the doors close.

"God speed," I hear one of them say behind me before they are gone.

God speed, indeed.

Running my fingers along the wall to keep my balance, I slowly make my way down the hall.

What is my room number, again?

1542?

That could be it. Let's try it.

I fish the key card out of my purse and swipe it against the door lock.

Red light.

Shit.

Try again.

Green light.

I breathe a sigh of relief, fall through the doorway and hit the floor. Kicking the door shut, I reach up and hold the doorknob for support to stand up and lock the door. I strip off my clothes, not even looking for my pajamas, and crawl into bed.

Please don't throw up. Please don't throw up.

My eyes shut.

There are ten text messages waiting for me when I open my eyes the next morning. Liz. Brittany. McGruff.

I flip my phone back onto the bedside table. I can't deal with that right now. My head is pounding, and I can barely keep my eyes open. But my bladder is full.

Son of a bitch. I have to move.

But I don't.

Gemma, you really need to pee.

Yep. Oh, wait did I puke last night?

I lift the covers. I'm only in my underwear. Hmm. No evidence of vomit.

Go to the bathroom.

Fine.

Gently and deliberately, I swing my legs out from under the covers and sit up.

Shit, my head.

It's fine. There's Tylenol in your bag in the bathroom.

Raising myself to my feet, I walk to the bathroom. No sign of puke here, either.

Well, I'll be damned.

You feel damned.

I do. Why did I do this to myself?

Because you over compensated and treated your anxiety with alcohol instead of braving it out.

Right.

But you did have fun. Didn't you?

My lips curve into a smile. Yes, I did.

CHAPTER FIVE

"So, this is our kick off meeting."

No. Stupid. They know it's the kick off meeting because it's the first one, and you literally wrote that in the meeting invite.

"Hey, everyone, welcome to the meeting."

Welcome to the meeting? Are you for real?

I drop my head to my chest, put my hands on my hips, and take a deep breath. Rolling my head around and up my left shoulder, I exhale and roll my head back down my right shoulder. I look at my reflection in my bathroom mirror.

What are you saying? Just say hi and then start the meeting like a normal person.

Normal? When am I ever normal?

"Hey, guys, so Carl asked me to run these meetings for him."

Better.

"Hi, so Carl wanted me to lead this process."

More formal. More assertive. More commanding.

Yeah, I can't say that.

How about, "So, let's start with the requirements?"

Okay, that works. Who is in this meeting, again?

Jack. For the love of God, why?

You know what? Just let Jack take control, you know he's going to anyway.

That's not really the point of me leading these meetings. Carl wants me actually to lead them and not let someone else. He wants to see that I am management material.

Are you, though?

Rude. I could be if I wanted.

But do you want to?

That is a good question.

I take my usual route to the office, into Sally's to say hi to her and Walter, get some hot tea, and walk down the street and into the office building. McGruff has an early presentation this morning, so he wasn't able to walk with me today. Sometimes, it is nice to walk alone. Just me and the crisp autumn air.

Just you and the constant honking of car horns and the daily panic attack after entering the building.

Trying to be positive here.

The first item to check off my list today is finishing the survey that the new VP Jacqueline sent out to get a better idea of the department, our needs, and our goals. All of the questions are pretty straight forward except for those about inclusion and diversity. I want to answer that people with anxiety should be treated differently...no not differently. It should be understood...no.

What are you trying to say?

That to be truly inclusive for people with diverse backgrounds, which includes people with anxiety, then...

Then, what?

I don't know! I don't want to say accommodate because that's not the right word. I just want to be able to work like other people work without feeling like I am going to die during the day because of a crushing weight on my chest because I have to go to a stupid meeting.

Because the office and company cater to outgoing and non-anxious individuals.

Exactly! I want to be able to work from home without someone thinking I am getting preferential treatment, when all I really want is to be normal, and I can only do that from home.

"Still haven't filled out the survey yet?"

I look up to see Brittany standing in front of my desk.

"When did you get here?" I ask.

"A few seconds ago. So, still working on the survey?"

"How'd you know?"

"You have quizzical face on."

"I don't know what to say."

"It is supposedly anonymous, so just say what you want to."

"Yeah." I sigh.

"Just write from the heart!" Nick yells through the partition.

"Oh, shut up," Brittany replies to him. She smiles and then darts off.

It's a good opportunity to say what you feel. It may be your only opportunity, so you should take it.

I know.

I type in that consideration should be made to help those with anxiety feel more at ease at work, for example working from home.

Not bad.

Wait. What is that? Why do I feel like I am going to puke? Why is my stomach getting progressively more upset? Is it the survey? I don't think so. Oh, wait.

It's time for my meeting with Jack. Yes, *my* meeting. My first of many meetings when I have to lead Jack. Yes, surely a reason to puke.

I hate that my body just knows. I don't even have to be thinking about the meeting, but it is unconsciously aware that time is ticking away and getting closer and closer to the dreaded meeting. It's not fair. If I'm not thinking about it, I shouldn't be anxious.

Anxiety is an over achiever.

I arrive to the conference room early, obviously. Jack comes in, sits directly across from me and grunts. I am assuming that is his greeting to me.

Damn it. Could he not sit somewhere else? Like in another meeting maybe?

Thankfully, Nick and Joe are also in here, along with Ed, my new bestie.

You know what? This may not be too bad after all.

"What are you doing in here?" Joe asks as he sits down. "I'm the BA on this project. Aren't I?"

"Yeah, you are. Carl wants me to run these meetings...like a project manager."

"Like a PM?" Joe, Ed, and Nick all say at once.

Surprise? Shock? Incredulity?

They probably don't believe you can do it.

Heck, I don't believe it, either.

"Yep. Have to put my knowledge from the conference to work, I guess."

Ed leans in and whispers in my ear, "Do you hate it?"

I say softly back, "Yes, I do."

"Okay!" Jack yells. "Enough wasting time. I wanted to start with this requirement."

I raise my palm in exasperation and the other three guys just shrug.

I suck so bad at this.

"You know, what?" Ed says. "That reminds me."

Do not say anything about me dancing. Please.

"It was my cat's birthday the other day."

Of course, it was.

"And we got her this new scratching post with catnip in it. She went crazy."

Take control of your meeting, Gemma.

"What?" Jack grunts. "How does that remind you of this requirement for the web?"

Ed whispers, "The part where she went crazy."

I can hear Nick snicker.

"So, this is how your meetings go, too?" I ask Joe.

"Oh, yes, without a doubt."

"You've got to be kidding me!" Jack shouts. "Does no one in this room want to work?"

That's a no.

We all silently look around the table at each other.

"Well, that's it!" Jack yells as he gets up and walks out the door, slamming it behind him.

All of our mouths drop open, and we sit in a moment of quiet before we all erupt into laughter.

"Well, I'll be damned," Ed says. "If I knew that's all it took to get him to leave a meeting, I would have done it a long time ago."

A weight is lifted off of my shoulders without Jack's presence. My anxiety is not that bad with these three guys. I actually like them all. Gosh. I'd actually say I'm friends with them.

Don't be too excited. I doubt Carl will be happy when he finds out that Jack stormed out of the first meeting that you officially ran. That's got to be a record.

"So, what do we do now?" Joe asks.

"I don't know," Nick replies. "We usually only do work in these meetings because either Jack or Carl is here to make us."

"Now Gemma is the boss," Ed says.

They all turn to look at me.

"You think I want to be running meetings to harass you guys? I trust you all to do your work."

"Is that what you learned at the management conference?" Nick jests.

"Yep. I learned to not manage."

"And how to gamble," Ed adds.

"What did you really learn?" Joe asks. "I really wanted to go."

"Ed?" I pass the question and look at him.

He puts his fingers to his chest, "Me? Little old me? I learned how to zipline."

"Brittany told me!" Nick replies.

"It was awesome. Even our little Gemma here did it. But oh, Joe, we did learn management stuff. As you can tell by Gemma and me absolutely taking control of this meeting and not letting anyone walk out."

"At least you aren't supposed to manage this meeting. I am," I say.

"Don't worry. We will all say you did until you can get yourself out of this mess," Ed replies.

By mess, does he mean the management track?

"So, it's unanimously agreed that we are taking Jack off of this meeting, right?" Nick asks.

"Oh, yes," Ed responds.

"Yep," Joe answers.

"Seriously, guys? I can't do that. I mean, I would love to, but Carl would kill me," I respond.

"Oh, Gemma," Ed whines.

Actually, how can I make that happen? How can I get rid of Jack without causing a problem? I am the leader for this project.

"Okay, guys, come up with a solution to Jack's part in this project, and I will remove him from the invite," I say.

"Oh, Gemma," Nick whines.

"I know, being management sucks," I say and roll my eyes.

"Can't we just vote him off?" Ed asks.

"I wasn't at the management conference," Joe replies, "but I'm pretty sure that's Management 101. You just get rid of the people you don't like."

"You know, that does sound familiar," Ed responds.

"Doesn't it, Gemma?" Nick asks.

"Guys, I would be the first person to vote Jack out, but I'm pretty sure Carl would fire me."

Look at you putting your foot down. Maybe you are management material after all.

We all turn as there is a knock on the door. Carl peeks his head in the room.

"Time is up, guys," he says, then adds, "Where's Jack?"

I look at Ed, who looks at Joe, who looks at Nick.

"He had a stomach problem," Nick says.

"Oh," Carl says and closes the door.

Laughing, we all shake our heads.

"That was the best answer," Joe offers.

"It won't hold up in every meeting, though," Nick responds.

"Okay, I will try to figure something out," I say.

"You're the best, Gemmy Gem," Ed replies.

How the heck are you going to get rid of Jack? There's no way.

Ed and Joe walk out of the room as Nick whispers to me, "You're Gemmy Gem now?"

"Apparently."

Ah, Gemma. Things are going to look up. Got a feeling. It wasn't too long ago that you wouldn't even be able to sit in a meeting with Jack. Now you just let him walk out.

That is progress?

For leading meetings, probably not. But for anxiety, your level is a few notches below what it used to be. And you did tell the guys they can't just vote Jack out. You never would have been able to do that a few months ago. Things are looking up.

Should I have asked Ed about Larry? Why hasn't anyone said anything about Larry quitting? Is it not happening? Did Ed lie?

Just play it cool for now. Finish out the day. Finish out the day without thinking about the meeting that just happened.

As if I could not think about that meeting.

Just breathe.

Inhaling, I pull up my inbox which has somehow accumulated ten new messages during that meeting.

Ugh. I hate emails. Why do people need so much?

The last unread email is from Barb.

"Hello, Germa," the first line reads.

Are you serious? She can't even spell my name correctly? It is literally in my email address. I hate people that can't even be bothered to spell my name right, especially when they want something.

Ha! Germa. That's kind of funny. You're like a female germ.

No! It's rude and disrespectful.

Oh, don't be a germa.

When the day finally rolls to a close. I am the first person at the elevator. As I push the button, Ed stops next to me and smiles.

"You beat me," he says.

"I usually beat everyone. I just cut and run."

"I like your style," he responds as the doors open, and we cram ourselves into the nearly full box.

Obeying the unwritten elevator rules, we remain silent for the descent. When the doors open, and we all flee the box, Ed looks at me and asks, "Same time, same place tomorrow?"

I frown. "Unfortunately."

Damn it, Gemma. You should have asked about Larry.

I was playing it cool!

"Gemma!"

Instinctively, I turn my head to see McGruff waving at me from the side of the lobby. I stop in my tracks to wait for the crowd behind me to pass before attempting to meet McGruff halfway, but before I do, I turn to wave at Ed.

"Hey! Is that McGruff?" Ed shouts.

My eyes pop wide open as Ed smiles, waves, and then walks out of the building with the crowd.

What the hell? Brittany must have told Ed about Nate's nickname. I'm going to have to kill her.

Or maybe you did when you were drunk.

Fair point.

Maybe McGruff didn't hear.

He stops next to me and raises an eyebrow.

"McGruff?" he asks.

I stare at him, wide-eyed for a moment before walking off in the direction of the door.

"Hey!" he yells as he catches up. "Who was that guy, and why did he call me McGruff?"

"Yep."

"How hard?"

"As hard as I can."

"Gemma!"

"What? It's one of my coping mechanisms."

"I don't like that. Look at your arm."

"It'll go away."

"Oh, my Gemma," he sighs.

"Are you going to tell me what's in the box?"

"Oh, yes," he says as he throws his hands into the air. "It's a desk!"

My eyes open wide. "A desk!"

"Yes! I didn't want you to have to crouch over on the couch anymore. Since it is a permanent work from home situation, I wanted you to be comfortable and professional."

"Thank you! I love it."

"You haven't even seen it."

"I don't care. I love it," I say and kiss him lightly on the lips. "Does it come with a chair?"

"Oh, shit! I forgot about a chair!"

"You're such a dummy," I say and smile.

"Yes, I am!"

"I'll be fine. I'll just use it like a standing work station. Those are all the rage now."

"No, don't worry. I will get you a chair."

"I'm not worried."

"Well, you should be because you are going to help me put this desk together."

"Right now?"

"Yes, right now. Do you have something better to do?"

"Well, maybe," I say and kiss him again.

"Yeah, this can probably wait."

CHAPTER SIX

"Can't we just go somewhere else?" I ask as I glance out the car window to watch the buildings pass by.

"We're almost there," McGruff answers and places his hand on my knee.

"So? Let's just go out to dinner, the two of us."

"I'm sure they will have food there."

"So? There will be too many people."

"Too many people for what? To eat?"

"To be around?"

Very convincing answer, Gemma.

"It is your vice president's retirement party. You have to show up, even if just for a little while."

The Toyota comes to a stop in front of the hotel. It's a large brick building with ivy winding up the sides.

I look at McGruff who says, "We have to get out."

Damn it. The driver drove exactly where I asked him to. It's so rude.

Closing the car door, I pat down my dress to get rid of the static electricity. McGruff walks to my side and grabs my hand.

"Ready?" he asks.

"No. Let's call the driver back."

"Gemma, it's not going to be that bad."

"What if it is?"

He turns so we are facing each other. "Okay, breathe in," he says, takes a deep breath, and holds it. "And breathe out," he says as he exhales. I do the same. "One more time. In…and out…"

I can feel my pulse slowing.

"Better?" he asks.

"Slightly," I say and grin.

Starting up the steps, he pulls my hand with him until I am forced to follow. Inside the door is a sign with the company's name and an arrow pointing left. We stop at the coat check, and I hand over my coat in return for a small piece of paper with a number on it. When we walk through the double doors to the event room, I immediately see Bob to my right, greeting people as they arrive.

Nope. Not me. Please don't see me.

But he does.

"Gemma!" Bob exclaims as he takes a step toward me. "So great of you to come."

I had an option to not come?

He shakes my and then McGruff's hand as I remain silent and then scurry away.

He knows who I am.

Of course, he does. You've been in meetings with him, and he's your VP. He ain't dumb. He didn't get to be VP based on his good looks.

"Gemma, you just ran away from him," McGruff says.

"Did you expect anything else?"

McGruff smiles and says, "I guess not."

The room is large enough for at least ten tables with ten chairs each and a dance floor in the middle. Two long tables are at either end of the room with cheese, crackers, fruit, and trays soon to be filled with dinner. All of the tables have spotless white tables cloths, surrounded by chairs with white cloth tied around the backs. Gold candle sticks and flowers are arranged in the center of the round tables. Half of the tables are already filled with guests. I glance around but cannot spot Brittany or Nick.

"This is so fancy," McGruff notes.

"We don't usually have such a big room. Must be due to all of the extra guests."

"Like me."

"Thank God for that."

"Directly to the drink table, I am guessing?"

"You guess correct."

He takes my hand as we pass through the crowd to stand in line. I opt for wine, while McGruff gets a beer. Those are the only two choices.

"What do you usually do at these things?" he asks me.

"I hide with Brittany and Nick. But I don't see them."

"Okay, why don't I head over to get some food while you scour the place for them, and we'll meet back at that table?" he says and points to an empty one in the corner of the room.

Man after my own heart.

"You got it," I say.

Sipping my wine, I weave in and out of the crowd until I spot Brittany in line for a drink at the other end of the room. I catch up to her as she is turning around with her own glass.

"Hey!" I say.

"Oh, my God! Yay! Thank God! I lost Nick after I went to the bathroom and then just got in line for booze. I see you're almost in need of a second already."

"A girl's got to do what a girl's got to do."

"Amen, sister."

Walking to the side of the room, away from the tables and the people, Brittany and I stand in front of the wall.

"I didn't realize so many people would be here," Brittany says.

"Me neither. I thought it would just be Bob's department and their guests, but it looks like he invited most of the company. I don't even know most of these people. Do you think he invited people from outside the company?"

"I wouldn't be surprised. I only got invited because I am Nick's guest."

I see the corner of her mouth curve up ever so slightly.

"Hey, ladies!" Ed comes walking over. "Obviously, I'd find you two hanging out back here against the wall where no one is."

"You still found us," Brittany says.

"Touché," he responds and turns to the woman on his right. "Marjorie, this is Brittany and Gemma, the two ladies I went to Foxwoods with." He turns back to us. "Ladies, this is my wife, Marjorie."

"It's very nice to meet you two," she says as she shakes both of our hands.

Wow. She is real. I mean, I knew Ed had a wife and that she wasn't a figment of his imagination, but I kind of always thought that was a possibility. But no. She is real. And she is very pretty. She has a sweet round face, big blue eyes, and red lips. Her dirty-blonde hair is just to her shoulders.

"Ed said he had the best time with you two," she continues.

"Stop it," Ed fakes embarrassment and waves his hand in the air.

"We did, too," Brittany replies. "It was a lot of fun."

"All righty, well I see you two are already ahead of us, so we must make our adieu and head over to the drink table," Ed says.

"See you later," I say.

"I can't believe Ed is our bestie now," Brittany says as Ed and his wife disappear into the crowd.

"I can. It seems almost like it was inevitable."

"He does make work less sucky," Brittany replies.

"Yes. He'd love to know that."

"Less sucky. We should put that on a T-Shirt for him."

"Honestly, I think he'd love that."

"Oh, he so would."

I look around at all of my coworkers mingling effortlessly with each other like nothing could be easier.

"I hate this," I say.

"I know. But at least we have each…" she trails off.

Turning to look at her, I ask, "You okay?"

"You've introduced McGruff to Nick?" Brittany asks.

"No, not yet. I'm not sure it's a good idea."

"Well, you're too late." She points across the room. "Looks like they've met."

McGruff and Nick are chatting next to one of the food tables. They are both holding a plate of food with one hand and gesticulating with the other.

"Oh no. Oh no."

"I'm sure it's fine," Brittany says. "Come on. I'll walk over with you."

Hesitantly, I follow her across the room. When we stop next to them, they both turn to look at us.

"Oh, hey ladies," Nick says.

"Hey," I softly say. "You've met?"

"Met?" Nick asks.

He and McGruff both stare at me.

"Yeah. This is Nate. Nate, this is Nick," I respond.

I can see the realization on both of their faces as they slowly turn to look at each other.

"I guess we have met, now," McGruff says. "It's nice to meet you, Nick. Officially."

"Same. Nice to meet you, too."

I side eye Brittany, and she shrugs.

"Anyway," McGruff says. "As I was saying, I stayed up late to watch the end of the Bruins game. Did you see when the guy blatantly tripped the goalie. I was so mad!"

"Yes!" Nick shouts. "I nearly jumped through the television. The ref didn't even call it!"

"I know!" McGruff yells.

I take a few steps back and whisper to Brittany. "I guess I'm not needed here."

"Guess not."

I do not like this. I do not like this one bit. This new friendship has to stop. I must stop it somehow.

Why? They're getting along and not fighting. Aren't you happy about that?

No. I have to make them stop talking. But how? Fake a heart attack? Fake my own death? Projectile vomit?

"Hey," Brittany whispers. "You okay?"

"No. Do you see them?"

"Yeah. I think it's great. Now, there won't be anything weird between you and Nick. He and Nate are buddies now. I thought you'd be happy."

"Happy? I guess I'm happy. This situation just feels weird."

"It will be fine. Come on, let's go get some more wine."

"Okay."

I tap McGruff's arm and let him know we're walking away, but he just gives me a nod and doesn't stop talking to Nick.

What the hell? I think I've lost McGruff to Nick. They're probably going to start dating now. I will lose my boyfriend and a pack member both at once. How did I let this happen?

You didn't let anything happen. It just happened. Deal with it. And there's no way McGruff is leaving you for Nick. Pull yourself together.

"Are you sure you're okay?" Brittany asks as I take a sip of my newly acquired glass of wine.

I sigh. "Yeah. This budding bromance is fine. Like you said, now any remaining weirdness between Nick and me will be gone. I mean, I think he likes Nate more than he likes me at this point. Look at them."

We both glance across the room as the two of them toss their heads back in laughter.

"I can't compete with that," I say.

"Which guy are we talking about now?"

"Both of them. Nate is going to edge me out of the pack and then start dating Nick."

Brittany laughs. "Oh, come on! If anything, Nate will just become part of the pack."

"I'm not sure that's better. I'd rather be ostracized or put out to pasture."

"It will be fine. I promise."

"Oh! By the way, we need to talk about how Ed knows Nate's nickname."

"Oh…"

But just then I get a text. Pulling my phone out of my purse, I see it's from McGruff.

What the…?

I glance across the room. Both of them are watching me as I open the text and read it out loud to Brittany.

"We decided that the four of us are going to a Bruins game."

I look at Brittany and then at the guys, who both give me a thumbs up.

"You were saying about this being fine?" I say to Brittany.

"It *will* be fine," she repeats. "I think they are waiting for your answer."

Answer? That wasn't even a question. It was a statement.

I slowly raise my hand and give a thumbs up. They both cheer and raise their arms over their heads and high five each other.

What have I gotten myself into?

"I knew I should have come alone tonight."

"This isn't bad. It might be fun."

"Maybe. I need some more wine."

But before I can turn, Bob has come up next to us. My heartbeat quickens, and my head feels like a hot air balloon ready to take off.

"Hi, guys," he says. "I'm glad you both could make it tonight. I'm really enjoying this party. It's nice to see everyone out of the office once in a while. Especially, to celebrate."

What?

Say something, Gemma.

Say what?

Thanks for inviting us?

No, that's dumb.

I'm glad you are retiring?

No!

"It's a great party," Brittany responds. "I really enjoy getting to know people outside of work."

That makes one of us. Can I slowly back away and make a run for the bar? I'm sure neither of them would notice. They know I'm not going to say anything, anyway.

No! You can't. Talk to them.

Nope. I'm just going to take a few steps back. And then some more. What's Bob going to do about it? He is retiring. He can't fire me anymore.

Just smile and nod.

"What about you, Gemma?" Bob asks.

Oh, shit. I have no idea what he is asking.

"Are you having fun?" Brittany answers my silent question.

"Oh, yes. Thank you for inviting us. It was nice that we could bring a plus one."

Was it nice, though? Why would you say that? That was so dumb.

"Yes. I wanted it to be more like a party than a work gathering. I think it makes the atmosphere lighter."

"I agree," I muster.

It makes it lighter until the dancing starts.

Is this the time when Bob realizes he has made a huge mistake in talking to me and silently and slowly backs away? Oh please, let it be the time.

"How was the conference you two went to last week?" Bob asks.

Oh, God no. More chit chat.

"It was a lot of fun," Brittany responds.

What would I do without this girl?

"Fun?" Bob questions.

Brittany stiffens and is silent.

Oh, no. This is bad. Code Red. Defcon One. Brittany is incapacitated. Immediate extraction requested.

"Yes, well you see they gave us each free tickets to the zipline and the go-carts," I say and smile. "But I am sure Brittany was talking about the management presentations. Those were so much fun."

Bob laughs. I made Bob laugh.

"I see," he says. "Well, if I knew it was going to be that much fun, I would have gone myself!"

I laugh. Oh, my goodness. I am laughing with Bob. I am laughing with my VP.

"Yeah, I'd never ziplined before. It was quite the experience. Have you?"

What. Are. You. Doing?

"No, I haven't. I am not sure I'd be able to. I give you a lot of credit. Anyway, I must go entertain the hordes. Have *fun*," he says, emphasizing fun like we have an inside joke.

Oh, my. Do I have an inside joke with Bob, now?

Brittany grabs my arm at the elbow once Bob finally leaves us. "Look at you, girl! Laughing it up with Bob."

"I don't know what came over me. I saw you freeze, and I knew I had to take over."

"Yeah, I'm sorry about that. I don't know why I said it was fun."

"Because it was!"

"Well, yeah. But I shouldn't have told your VP that."

"Ah, who cares. He is no longer my VP, anyway."

"Good point. Sorry I froze."

"It's okay. You deserve to freeze every once in a while. You are always saving my ass."

"What about asses?"

"Oh, my God, Ed, what timing you have," Brittany says.

"I know!" he says over his shoulder as he passes us by.

Shrugging, I look at Brittany and say, "Less sucky."

"Less sucky, indeed."

McGruff catches my eye from across the room and points his index finger twice quickly to the open table in the corner.

"That's our cue," I say to Brittany.

"Cue?"

"Time to eat."

"But we don't have any food."

"We will."

Ignoring Brittany's inquiring look, I walk toward the corner of the room with Brittany following closely behind. As we approach, I can see that the guys each have two plates full of food in their hands. I turn to glance at Brittany, who shrugs in response.

"All right, ladies," Nick says as he places the dishes onto the table. "We've got pasta carbonara, chicken alfredo, and Nate over there has a plate of salad and one with roasted chicken and potatoes. We also snagged four rolls."

"This is amazing," Brittany says. "Did everyone else take this much?"

"Oh, no," Nick says. "But we braved the nasty looks."

"Well, thank goodness you are that brave," Brittany responds.

"How are we supposed to eat them?" I ask.

"Right!" McGruff pulls knives and forks out of his pocket, handles down of course, and takes the plates that he has tucked underneath his arm and puts them on the table.

"Armpit plates," I say.

"Only the best for my girl," he replies.

"Family style?" Brittany asks.

"Yep!" Nick says. "Take what you want."

"Pack dinner," Brittany says.

I stop mid reach. Pack dinner? I glance over at Brittany and then at Nick. Are we including McGruff in this pack now? Do I say something? Do I stay frozen like this forever, in a perpetual reach for pasta?

"Pack dinner," Nick repeats.

I let out the breath that I didn't know I was holding and resume my reach for the chicken alfredo and scoop some onto my armpit plate. When the pasta is in place, I reach over and touch McGruff's knee and squeeze. He puts his own hand on mine.

"I saw you talking to Bob," he says to me.

"Yeah, it surprised me too," I respond.

"She was amazing!" Brittany adds. "She made Bob laugh!"

"Yeah, Gemma!" Nick says. "Finally getting good with Bob."

"Yeah, now that he's retiring," I say and laugh.

"I'm still proud of you," McGruff says and smiles sweetly.

As we finish eating, Nick exclaims, "Oh, my God! It's time. I was not prepared for it this early!" Panicked, he looks at me.

"No!" I respond. "It can't be! We just finished eating."

"It'll be okay," Nick says. "Just don't look directly at it."

"I have to, though! But I can't at the same time!"

McGruff looks at Brittany and asks, "Do you have any idea what they are talking about?"

"Yes! This time I do!" she shouts and points to the dance floor where our coworkers have already gathered to publicly humiliate themselves.

You mean dance.

Same thing.

"Oh," McGruff says and scratches his chin. "It does seem a bit early for the spectacle of lights."

The three of us turn to look at him.

"Spectacle, obviously," he responds and points to the dancing coworkers. "Lights…light weight drinkers. That's what the guys and I call them when they start dancing at our company parties, the spectacle of lights."

Definitely pack member material.

"All right, guys," the DJ's voice booms across the room. "We don't usually do this at company parties, but since I've been advised this is a plus-one crowd, we are going to slow it down for you. Let's see all those plus-ones out there!"

No. Nope. Do not like this.

Surprisingly, the tables start to empty as most of my coworkers take to the floor to slow dance.

"Should we?" Nick asks.

"Yes!" Brittany replies.

Getting up, they both smile at my horrified gasp and saunter out onto the floor.

"I don't know why I was so worried about you and Nick a few months ago. Look at the two of them," McGruff says.

Yes, look at them, all cozy dancing cheek to cheek.

Seriously, what does it matter to you?

It doesn't.

Are you sure? Because you get all snarky every time someone brings them up.

I don't get snarky.

Okay, right there. That was snarky.

Yeah. I haven't figured it out yet.

"Well?" McGruff questions.

"I swore to myself I would never dance at a work function."

"This is slow dancing. It doesn't count. All we do is just sway. If anyone does anything weird, it won't be us, and we will immediately vacate the dance floor. Look. Literally everyone else is doing it."

Yes, really. Everyone else is doing it.

I open my mouth but immediately close it.

McGruff leans in to listen.

"I guess," I whisper.

He smiles. "Good. Let's show these IT guys and gals how to sway."

"Let's not. Let's just hide in the crowd."

"Or that. That works for me."

He takes my hand and leads me out onto the floor that is already covered with coworkers snuggled up to their plus-ones.

This is gross. Now I see why we never get plus-ones. It is just weird seeing them like this. I don't want to think of them as having lives other than sitting at a desk all day. I don't want to see them dancing with their wives and husbands. I was happier not knowing anything about their lives.

Seriously? They are people, too.

I can feel McGruff's hand on my waist as I lean into his chest.

Everyone is thinking that about you too, you know.

Let them. I am surprisingly content dancing with my McGruff in the midst of all of my colleagues.

"See, this isn't so bad," McGruff whispers to me.

"Pretty nice, actually."

CHAPTER SEVEN

Oh, my head. I didn't drink *that* much last night.

It's because of your medication, remember? It compounds the effect of alcohol.

Ugh, yes. Somehow, I never care until it bites me in the ass.

I roll my head to the side only to find an empty pillow where McGruff should be.

What is that noise? No, wait. It's music coming from outside the bedroom.

Time to get up, Gemma. You can do it. Follow the noise.

Lifting the comforter, I pull my legs out and my feet hit the floor. My hands instinctively reach for my forehead.

I should have just stayed in bed.

Welp, you're up now. Might as well go out.

Slowly, I open the door and creep out. McGruff is sitting in a wooden chair with his back to me. A record player is spinning out jazz music. McGruff raises both his arms in the air and leans to the left and then to the right.

Ah, he's doing senior tai chi like we do with Walter in the Boston Common in nice weather.

It's called chair tai chi, not senior tai chi.

He stops and turns around when he hears me.

"Morning," he says.

"Hey," I respond and shuffle over to the couch and flop down. "You're lively this morning."

"Yeah, I like tai chi. It relaxes me," he says, stands up, and walks to the kitchen. "I've been waiting for you to get up. I made myself breakfast. I will finish making yours now."

McGruff places a dish on the kitchen table, on it are scrambled eggs and toast.

"That's so far away," I say.

"Come on, you can do it."

"I don't think I can."

He places a cup of coffee next to the dish. "How about now?"

"Okay, I'll give it a shot," I say, launch myself off of the couch, shuffle over to the table, and sit.

"You're lucky you have me to cook you breakfast," he says.

"What? I can make toast and eggs."

Can you?

"Can you?" he playfully asks.

"Yes."

"Well, I was thinking that the two of us could go to one of those cooking nights where they teach you how to cook a meal."

"Are you saying I can't cook?"

Yes. That's exactly what he is saying.

"All I'm saying is that since Sally's is no longer open for dinner, it might be nice to learn how to make a new meal."

"Because I can't cook?"

"There will be wine. And we get to eat the meal after. It will be a nice date."

"Okay. You had me at wine."

He awkwardly smiles.

I know what he is thinking. I drink too much. But I don't.

You sure? You just dragged your butt out of bed, and he looks like he's been up for hours.

Letting out a huge sigh, I lean my head against my hand and prop it up with my elbow on the table. Picking up the fork, I shovel in some eggs.

"How much wine did you have last night?" he asks.

And there it is.

"A few glasses."

"Gemma…" He looks at me with concerned blue eyes.

"I know, I know."

He, again, smiles awkwardly and leans back in his chair as he takes a sip of coffee.

"Last night was actually fun," I say as I take a bite of toast.

"Yeah. I really like your coworkers. Nick and Brittany are so nice."

Yeah, yeah. They're super cool.

"I can't wait to go to a Bruin's game with them," he continues. "We should settle on a day."

That's happening? I was pretty sure that was a fever dream.

"What's that face for?" he asks.

"Nothing. Just seems like you and Nick got pretty chummy last night."

"Yeah. I really like him. I can see why you and Brittany hang out with him."

Okay. Cool. So, no longer jealous?

Why do you want him to be jealous? There is nothing going on with Nick. You don't want anything to happen with Nick. Why are you being weird about them becoming friends?

"Yeah, he's pretty cool," I say.

"Brittany is, too. She reminds me of Liz a little."

"People like them just seem to adopt me. Present company included."

McGruff grins. "You're kind of likeable."

"Just kind of."

"But Gem…"

Uh oh.

"I know you don't like it when I bring it up…"

Not this again.

"But you really shouldn't be drinking that much while on your meds. It's not good for you. Look at you right now."

Harsh.

"I know…I know."

But really, look at you. Is there a mirror in here? You probably look like crap.

There is a knock on the door. McGruff's eyes dart to the door and then back to me. His whole body tenses.

Uh oh. What the hell is happening?

Quickly standing up, McGruff promptly goes to the door and opens it. He stands up straight like he's at attention.

What the heck? What is happening over there?

I get up out of the chair and stand awkwardly next to the table and my half eaten breakfast.

I should have eaten it all. Why didn't I eat it all? I have a feeling I won't be able to now.

"You're early," McGruff says to whoever is standing on the other side of the door.

"We left earlier than expected," a woman's voice softly says.

"Are you going to let us in?" a man's voice gruffly asks.

"Yes," McGruff answers and steps aside.

A man and a woman enter, look around, and both pairs of eyes land on me.

Holy shit. Are these his parents? That's his dad? The same dad who made my poor McGruff anxious and need control in every aspect of his life? The dad I had prayed never to meet because he sounds so confident and the complete opposite of myself?

My heartbeat races. Do I salute? Do I curtsy? Do I pretend like I'm his maid? Maybe burst into song like a medieval court troubadour? I think I just peed my pants.

"Honey," McGruff's mom says and touches his arm. "Who is this?"

Shit. They spotted me. Why can I never be invisible when I want to be? For the love of goodness, I should be able to will myself into invisibility by now.

"Mom, Dad, this is Gemma," McGruff answers. He seems hesitant. Why is he hesitant? Is he embarrassed by me? Does he not want me to meet them? Heck. That's fine. I would rather not meet them, honestly. I should just leave. They are kind of blocking the doorway, but I think I can hip check my way through. Or do these windows open? Maybe there's a fire escape nearby?

"Oh, my God. You're beautiful," his mom says, walks towards me with her arms extended, and hugs me.

Oh, my God. This is happening. McGruff's mom is hugging me.

I peek over to see McGruff's dad glaring at me.

Oh, shit. I made eye contact.

You really should have looked in a mirror this morning.

McGruff's mom lets go and looks at me. "It's so nice to meet you," she says. "You can call me Jen."

Jen? I can call her Jen? How about Mrs. Parker? That seems more appropriate, right? Because his dad is certainly not going to tell me to call him by his first name. It will be Mrs. and Sargent Parker from now on.

"It's nice to meet you, too," I respond.

She motions towards her husband. "This is Thomas."

He reaches out his hand.

Oh, shit. He's going to judge my handshake.

I slowly put my hand into his.

"Nice to meet you, sir," I say.

Sir? Really? You called him sir?

Well, I sure as shit ain't going to call him Thomas. And, of course, he's a Thomas and not a Tom. Look at him. He is so no-nononsense. I bet he's judging me right now.

Oh, for certain he is. For starters you're in your jammies and you haven't brushed your hair.

He is taller than McGruff, maybe 6'4" so he looms over all of us. His crystal blue eyes show no emotion as he responds, "You, as well." His posture is impeccable and his dark hair is still in a crew cut, presumably, from his military days.

McGruff's mom, on the other hand, is shorter than me, maybe 5 foot 4 inches, and her dark brown eyes are soft and welcoming with crow's feet at their corners. Her light brown hair is curled and to her shoulders. She smiles at me.

"Nate has told me so much about you. I was hoping we'd get to meet you this weekend."

What? Why was I not informed of this weekend?

"I was, too," I respond.

I hope Sir Thomas can't smell lies because it kind of feels like he can smell lies.

"So, I was thinking," Jen continues as Sir Thomas remains stoic in the background. "That we could go into Salem for the day today. How much fun would that be?"

Salem in October? A few days before Halloween? I could not think of anything less fun. Everyone knows that being in Salem in the month of October is an absolute shitshow. There are crowds everywhere, with almost nowhere to walk. All the shops and museums and pop-up haunted houses will be packed with people. The restaurants are probably full to the brims. Who in their right mind would want to go to Salem during Halloween month?

"That sounds great," McGruff says. "Right, Gemma?"

Me? I have to go?

"Yes," I respond and fake a smile.

"Great!" Jen exclaims. "It will be just like old times when we would go every year for your birthday, honey," she says to McGruff.

Birthday?

My eyes immediately dart to McGruff who smiles at me.

"We would all dress up for Nate's birthday and head into Salem," Jen explains to me. "It is our tradition. I am so glad you can join us this year. I can't believe our boy's birthday is in two days already."

Jen turns to Sir Thomas who nods back at her.

I look pleadingly at McGruff.

"Okay," he says. "Gemma, why don't you go home and get ready. I'll text you later, and you can meet us at North Station to get the train to Salem."

Oh, thank God he understands my looks.

"Sounds like a plan," I respond and move towards the door.

"Gem…" McGruff says and hurriedly grabs my purse from the couch and points at my shoes on the floor.

You were literally going to leave in your bare feet and without your purse and coat, weren't you?

Of course, I was! I completely forgot what was happening and lost all sense of reason. I still want to, but now that McGruff pointed out my mistake, it seems even stupider.

Absolutely stupid either way.

I slip on my high heels, because they are what I wore to the party last night and take my purse from McGruff's hand as he wraps my coat around me.

You look ridiculous. How is this their first impression of you?

"It was nice to meet you both. I will see you later," I sort of mumble and try to elegantly walk in my heels and pajamas to the door.

McGruff walks with me into the hallway and closes the door behind us.

"I'm so sorry," he says. "I didn't know they'd show up so early."

"Why didn't you tell me they were coming?"

"I did tell you."

"When?"

"When we video chatted while you were at Foxwoods."

Oh, shit. What else did he tell me when I was drunk as a skunk?

This is not good, Gemma.

"You okay?" he asks.

"Yes."

"You look adorable by the way."

"Oh, shut up. I look so dumb right now."

He kisses my forehead. "I will text you," he says and disappears back into his apartment.

I look down at my pj pants and heels.

Just great. McGruff's parents arrive, and here I am looking like a fool.

Did you know it was his birthday?

No! I can't believe McGruff didn't tell me that it was his birthday. Who does that?

You would definitely do that.

Okay, yes, I would. But McGruff? He's so much more normal than I am. Why wouldn't he want me to know it's his birthday?

Maybe he told you when he told you that his parents were coming to visit.

Oh, God. I forgot everything important!

Nope. Calm down. Maybe it just didn't come up. Does he know when your birthday is?

Probably not.

See.

But mine is also not in two days.

Fair point.

What do I get him as a present? I have to get him one, right? That's what girlfriends do?

Yes, you have to get him one.

But, what?

He said something while you were on the phone with him at Foxwoods. What was it?

What was it? Shit if I know. I was drunk. I didn't even remember him telling me that his parents were coming to town.

It was something that he liked. Just think.

Nope. There's nothing there. Where there should be a memory there is just a dark void.

What about concert tickets?

I guess I could look.

Bruins tickets?

Buy the tickets to the game that I've been thinking about how to get out of going to?

Yes, those.

Fine.

And you have to buy four tickets.

Yeah, I know.

And invite Brittany and Nick. Not Liz and Brett.

Ugh. Fine.

Text them right now to see when they are free.

Now?

Yes. His birthday is in two days.

Fine.

Taking my phone out of my purse, I first order a car, and then I send a group text to Brittany and Nick.

Please respond that neither wants to go and are busy for the rest of their lives.

Why are you so against going to this game with them?

As I ride down the elevator, I think about that question. Why am I? I don't have feelings for Nick. Is it just that two worlds are colliding?

If that's the reason, then get over it.

Trying. Never in my life have I ever been able to just get over anything.

Brittany responds first. "Absolutely!"

Nick replies soon after. "You'd better believe it!"

Wait a second. Is it weird that I'm buying him tickets and then forcing him to go with my own friends and not his?

Now that you mention it, yes.

Brittany texts again, "How about next weekend?"

Nick responds, "Yes!"

Okay, well it's too late now. It's happening.

As I am opening the door to my apartment after my Road Trip home, my phone dings.

McGruff's text reads, "My parents are going to stay here for a little bit while they wait for check-in time at their hotel. Once they check in, we're going to take the train into Salem, walk around, and have dinner."

That sounds like a plan…that doesn't include me. He said nothing about me, right? I don't have to go?

A follow-up text says, "We will meet you at North Station at three."

Oh, man. There's the confirmation. I have to go.

Did you really think you were getting out of going? They told you as you left McGruff's apartment that you were going with them.

A girl can dream.

You should probably respond to him.

I sigh and send a thumbs up emoji.

Another text comes in. "It will be fine, Gemma. We will have each other."

I feel like even if McGruff's mom joined our side, we'd still be no match for Sir Thomas.

Absolutely. He would crush you all with his bare hands.

I wonder if this is how McGruff has felt his entire life. I've known the man for less than an hour, well a couple of minutes applied time, and I am an anxious mess. No wonder McGruff feels the need to be in control all of the time. If he didn't, he would probably fall apart from the might of the anxiety like I am about to do right now. And I just met the man.

Pull it together, Gemma.

But I don't. My stomach turns and my heart races. My head gets light.

What are you doing? Look at yourself. You have hours before you need to see Sir Thomas again, and you are already a hot mess.

I wish my anxiety was like McGruff's. Instead of coming apart at the seams, I'd rather reign it in and push it down and away until it forced me to need control over everything.

That doesn't sound all that much better. It actually may be healthier to let it out than to stomp it down like it doesn't exist.

I'm not sure either of us have any control over how we react. I know I don't.

What are you going to do for the next few hours while you wait?

Have a panic attack.

No, you should relax.

But I don't. I nervously clean my apartment, shower, and flop down onto the couch.

Should I go to Sally's?

You can't handle coffee today. You are already too anxious to even attempt normal human interaction. You can't add caffeine to the mix, especially when you need to face Sir Thomas again.

But maybe Walter will be there?

What would Walter do for you?

I don't know. How about chair tai chi?

Wouldn't hurt.

Pulling my desk chair, which I ordered online, out from the desk and into the middle of the room, I sit with my back straight and with my knees over my ankles.

Good. Just breathe.

Head rolls. Touch the sky. Shooting the bow. Golden lion shakes its mane.

There. Do you feel better?

Yes, I do.

Good because it's time to call a Road Trip. You need to meet McGruff's parents at the train station.

Nope. Going to throw up. Benefits of tai chi defeated by the beast.

You can do this.

I have to do this.

Quelling my nausea with the fresh air of outside, I wait for the car to pick me up outside my apartment building. I get inside and close my eyes for most of the journey.

Oh no. Oh no. I'm almost there.

It will be okay. Calm down.

But I don't. My hands shake as I unlock my seat belt, open the car door, and stand on the curb in front of North Station, which also happens to share the same space as the TD Garden, formerly the Boston Garden.

I pass a statue of a hockey player leaping into the air. The plaque states it is Bobby Orr's famous Stanley Cup winning goal. Pulling open the door, I try to steady my hand.

You're fine! Just breathe. McGruff will be there. Jen seems very nice. It's just Sir Thomas that you have to worry about. Just avoid him at all cost.

I slowly breathe in and then exhale as I approach the station. There's a huge board on the wall with departure and arrival times, as well as information on if the trains are on time. The numbers one through ten are written above each of the openings to train bays. I catch my breath when I see the three Parkers standing in a line in the open space in front of the opening to bay seven. All of the benches are occupied and travelers loiter all over the room, even sitting on the floor, waiting for trains.

There's still time. You can go home. No one has seen you. Just disappear back into the crowd, never to be seen again.

"Gem!"

I look up to see McGruff holding his arm in the air and waving at me. His mom smiles, and his father glares.

Well, this should be fun.

You can still turn around. You are far enough away so that they can't catch you. Turn and run!

But I don't. Hesitantly, with my heart racing, I step forward, and inexplicably, keep going until I am standing in front of McGruff.

"Hey, you," he says.

I silently stare up at him as he leans in for a kiss. Quickly, I turn my head so his lips land on my cheek.

Oh my God, Gemma. So awkward.

What was I supposed to do? Kiss him right in front of his parents?

Yes, that is what you were supposed to do.

Well, I never do what I'm supposed to do, now do I?

McGruff slides his hand around my waist.

Don't you dare push him away!

"Here, I got your ticket," he says and hands me a small rectangular piece of paper.

"Thank you."

"How was your day, Gemma?" Jen asks.

Oh, I spent the whole day worrying about this exact situation and the one about to commence.

"It was good. Thank you. How was yours?"

"Great. We checked into the hotel. Our room is lovely. Don't you think, Thomas?"

Sir Thomas cooly looks down at his wife and says, "It is."

And I thought *I* wasn't a big talker.

McGruff holds my hand and lightly squeezes it.

"Have you ever been to Salem, Gemma?" Jen asks.

"Yes, but not during Halloween season."

"Oh, you'll love it!"

I doubt that. I've heard things, nightmarish things, and not Halloween things. People things.

"We used to go every year for Nate's birthday," Jen continues. "It was our tradition. I wonder if our favorite restaurant is still there."

"It's not, Mom. I checked."

"Oh, too bad. I always loved it there."

Holy hell. Can our train arrive, please? I can't take anymore small talk standing next to McGruff's dad, who I can feel judging me with his crystal blue eyes.

Must be where McGruff got his eyes from. It's so strange to see such different emotions coming from such similar eyes.

"Our train," Sir Thomas says flatly.

Holy crap. He won't even talk in complete sentences. Maybe this is something I should adopt. Seems to work for him.

I look up to see the number four next to the train line we need to get on. A flock of people speeds towards the opening to the track as McGruff pulls my hand, and I follow the Parkers down the track and into a train car. The men let Jen and me in first, so I walk behind Jen as she decides the best place to sit. I see her eyeing four seats, but one set is flipped backward, so that they are facing each other.

Please no. Please don't sit there.

But she does. She takes a seat by the window as I sit down directly across from her. The two men take their respective places next to us.

"This is going to be so much fun," Jen says.

I look at McGruff and then at Sir Thomas. Yep. I am in the majority. She is not.

McGruff slides his hand over to take mine, but I pull it away and cross my arms over my chest.

What gives, Gemma?

I don't know! I feel weird around Sir Thomas.

Take McGruff's hand. You will feel better.

And I do. I put my hand in his and give him an apologetic look. He winks at me.

See, don't you feel better?

Yes, I do.

Looking out the window, I watch as the train pulls away from the station and out into the city, passing highways and the Zakim Bridge.

"Here we go," Jen says, her eyes lighting up.

Yep, here we go.

Thankfully and horrifyingly, we sit in silence for the entirety of the train ride. Is it that Jen doesn't want to talk and Sir Thomas is not a talker? Or do they not like me? Well, I know Sir Thomas doesn't.

Shush. It's just too loud to make conversation.

I glance over to McGruff, who gently smiles back at me. When I turn back to face the window, I feel him lightly squeeze my hand.

Silence is for the best. I can't imagine having to talk right now.

The muffled voice of the train conductor over the intercom says something that I assume is, "Salem," since Sir Thomas and McGruff start to stand as the train screeches to a halt.

"We need to go straight down Washington Street and then take a left onto Essex Street," Sir Thomas commands. "Essex Street doesn't allow cars, so people are allowed to walk about freely."

I don't know if those directions are for me, since I've never been with them before in Salem, or for all of us because he needs to be in charge.

When we turn to Essex Street, I stop for a moment and take in the sight of the cobble stone streets and the brick buildings. People dressed as witches, goblins, and everything in between swarm the walk ways. I can't tell who is a tourist, a towny, or an employee at one of the shops. There are so many people, the street is blocked by bodies. I don't know how we will even walk down there. It is a moving wall of humans.

"This is your first time in Salem at Halloween, Gemma?" Jen asks.

"Yeah, I haven't been here for a while and never this close to Halloween."

"It's a trip, right?" she asks.

"Oh, yes."

McGruff takes my hand and squeezes it, again. Is it possible that he can feel my heart beating faster as every person bumps me on their way past us?

Just breathe! Please don't have a panic attack in front of McGruff's parents.

It's no longer a matter of will a panic attack happen; it is a matter of when it will happen.

"Just breathe," McGruff whispers into my ear.

"Should we get dinner first?" Jen asks.

"Honey, I don't think we'll be able to get into any restaurant right now," Sir Thomas advises.

Honey? A term of endearment coming from his lips surprises me. Maybe he's not that bad, after all? It could be that he is reserved around other people.

Like you.

"Why don't we scope out those food trucks over there?" McGruff suggests. "Probably more likely to get food there than in any of these restaurants anytime soon."

My chest tightens like rope is being wound around my heart. I start to feel dizzy and my breathing shallows. Putting my hand to my head, I close my eyes.

Oh, my God. I'm going to pass out. Please don't do this. Please don't do this. Not here. I will get trampled.

Air, Gemma. Get some air. Move to a less crowded area. Go!

"Gemma?" I barely hear McGruff ask before I shakily veer off out of the crowd.

"I'll be right back!" I faintly hear him yell as I reach a less populated alleyway, put my palm against a brick wall, lean over, and take deep breaths. I feel McGruff's hands slide across my back.

"Gemma, are you okay?"

I can only shake my head.

"Okay, honey, just breathe. Listen to my voice. Ready? Breathe in one, two, three. Breathe out one, two, three. One more time. Breathe in one, two, three. And out one, two, three."

Still with my hand against the wall, I stand up straight, and breathe in.

"Good," he says and puts his palm on my cheek. "Good. Look at me."

My eyes connect with his hypnotizing blue, concerned eyes.

"We okay, now?" he asks.

I take another deep breath. "Yeah, we're okay now."

He kisses me softly on the forehead.

Taking another deep breath, I breathe out and lean into him, nuzzling my face into the crook of his neck. He slides his hand up my back and rests it on the nape of my neck with a palm full of my hair.

"Ready to go back?" he asks.

"Do we have to?" I reply without moving my face from his neck.

"I really want to say no, but I think we have to, yeah."

Breathing in the scent of his cologne, I inhale and pull myself away from him. Looking into his eyes, I say, "Okay."

He smiles. "No push back at all?"

"No. They're your parents. I understand, we have to go back to them."

Even if neither of us wants to.

Grabbing my hand, he leads me back through the crowd and to his parents, who are waiting right where we left them.

"Are you okay?" Jen asks, coming over to me and placing her hands on my elbows.

"Yes, thank you. I just got a little claustrophobic. I'm sorry about that."

"No need to apologize, dear," she says and smiles. "Right, honey?" she asks Sir Thomas.

No need to involve him. I'm sure he sees both my anxiety and my apology as signs of weakness.

Sir Thomas doesn't respond to the question, but instead suggests, "Nate, why don't you go get her a bottle of water. It might make her feel better."

"No, it's fine, really," I say.

He doesn't look at me or even acknowledge my words. He only says sternly, "Nate."

"Yes, I'm on it."

Huh. I didn't expect that from Sir Thomas. Is that how he shows that he cares? He tries to make you feel better not by words, but by actions? Does that mean he likes me?

Don't get ahead of yourself, Gemma. He didn't even notice that you spoke.

"I'll come with you," Jen offers and follows after McGruff.

No! Nope. Please no. Please don't leave me here alone with Sir Thomas. Oh, no. What do I say? We are just standing here in awkward silence. What could I possibly say to this man?

How about them Bruins?

No, definitely not that.

I like your hair cut?

No! Why would you even say that?

Your wife is nice.

Oh, Gemma! No.

My heart speeds up. I think I'm going to have another panic attack. Why did McGruff leave me like this?

Because his father ordered him to go.

You can do this. You talked to Bob at his retirement party. For goodness' sake, you made him laugh! You can do this!

"I don't like crowds, either," Sir Thomas offers.

I hold my breath and slowly turn my eyes in his direction. Did he just speak to me? And is he trying to make me feel better and relate to me?

Yes! Say something! Respond!

"I didn't realize the streets and sidewalks would be so crowded. There is no room to move," I say.

He doesn't respond.

Damn it, Gemma. Why'd you say that?

I don't know! Did I say too much? Did I say too little? Did I say something stupid?

"He's a good kid."

What? Is he speaking again? To me? Is he talking about McGruff? To me?

"I know I'm hard on him," he continues without ever turning to look at me. Awaiting the return of McGruff and Jen, we both continue to face forward as he goes on. "I just can't help it sometimes. I know how great and extraordinary he can be. I try to bring that out in him. But maybe I do it the wrong way."

Oh, my God! Is this really happening? Is he really saying these things out loud to me? I'm not hallucinating, am I? Oh, my God, do I respond? What do I say? What can I say? Yeah, you are hard on him, maybe stop? No, I can't say that. Just agree that he is great?

No, that's so dumb. He's pouring his heart out here, and look at you, you are just standing here awkward and silent.

That's what I usually do.

Well, be better!

My body relaxes a little when I see McGruff making his way through the crowd to us.

"He's a really good man," Sir Thomas finishes saying just as McGruff comes into earshot.

"I got us all a water," McGruff says and hands each of us a bottle.

Sir Thomas looks at me for the first time and says, "See."

He immediately looks away, but is that a crooked smile I see? Oh, my God. He does love his son.

Of course, he does! Why did I ever think he didn't?

Because McGruff told you how tough he is on him and that he caused anxiety for his whole life.

Oh, right. Well, I have to explain this conversation to McGruff later. Maybe it will help.

Will it help or hurt?

I think it will help. I see now how his father loves. It's not a conventional love, but it is love, and I think McGruff needs to know.

I'm sure he already knows. He just needs to be reminded.

"Feeling better, Gemma?" Jen asks.

"Yes, a little, thank you. Sorry for acting like this."

"No need to apologize, dear. Salem a few days before Halloween is enough to make anyone run for cover!"

"Are you ready to walk?" McGruff asks me.

"Yes. I am fine."

"I have an idea," Sir Thomas says. "Why don't we get some food from those food trucks, as you suggested, son, and then walk down to Pickering Wharff and sit by the water. There are probably less people down there."

"I'll be fine, I don't want to ruin your usual trip."

"We don't have a usual now that our restaurant is gone," Jen says.

"Good," Sir Thomas says, and then he slightly turns to me and adds, "follow behind me."

Holy Moly. Did we just become best friends?

Sir Thomas just offered to part the Red Sea for me.

I can't believe this. I am sure it's just because of my panic attack, but still. He is not at all what I imagined. I mean, he is terrifying, but also sweet in his own way. I guess McGruff, being his son, doesn't get that or doesn't see that side of him. Maybe it's because I'm a girl.

Following closely behind Sir Thomas, we weave around the crowd, and each of us gets a food truck burrito before being directed towards Pickering Wharff.

An old wooden ship is docked there, *The Friendship*. It is beautiful. I count nine sails and three masts. The body is painted black with gold trim. We sit at a bench overlooking the wharf and the ship.

"Much better, right, Gemma?" Jen inquires.

"Yes, thank you all."

As I unwrap my burrito, I ask, "Do you usually go to the haunted houses?"

"Usually, yes," Jen says.

"Are you up for that?" McGruff asks.

From their faces, I can tell they generally look forward to the haunted houses.

"Yes!" I shout.

"Great!" Jen says.

I really just want to see Sir Thomas demolish everyone in his path in one of those houses. Or maybe he just silences the monsters with an icy glare. The ghosts are probably scared of him.

Oh. My. God. You like him.

I see the corner of Sir Thomas' mouth turn up.

"You sure?" McGruff whispers into my ear.

"I am so sure."

Standing up from the bench, Sir Thomas shouts, "Onward march!"

What? Right now? I'm not done with my burrito.

Looks like you are.

I glance at McGruff, who downs the rest of his and jumps to his feet. He looks at me, opens his eyes wide, and nods his head towards his dad.

I guess when Sir Thomas says we move, we move.

Yeah, Gemma, go!

I was really enjoying this burrito.

Well, it's over now. Swallow it whole.

"Follow me," he says, and we all fall in line behind him like a military march through enemy territory.

Why are we walking so fast? I can barely keep up.

You're in the military now, Gem.

Nope. Back to being anxious. Why do I feel like I'm in boot camp?

Because you are. Now walk faster.

"This one," he shouts and veers off down an alley with us all trailing behind.

It's an alley. Literally an alley. With a random door into a building. Is this even a haunted house?

I tug at McGruff's sleeve.

"It'll be okay," is all he says.

Really? Has he seen the haunted house that his father has chosen? This is not a Halloween haunted house. This is an actual haunted house in an alleyway off the grid in Salem. This may actually be someone's house. And like I said, obviously, haunted.

Sir Thomas hands over some cash to a man standing by the door. The man has long, knotted black hair. Honestly, it may be a wig. It may not. His clothes are in tatters.

This isn't a haunted house. Sir Thomas has just paid a man to kill you.

Stop it!

Sir Thomas opens the door, stands back, and motions us to go in before him.

Yep, this is definitely where you die.

Clutching McGruff's arm like my life depended on keeping my grip, I walk into the dark room.

Your life does depend on it.

I have no idea if McGruff's parents are behind us or not. It is so dark in this house. The walls seem to be too close for a normal room. Each room has oddly placed old wooden furniture and either dummies or real people standing in the corners.

"Ah!!" one creature yells as we pass by.

I grab McGruff's whole body.

"It's okay," he whispers.

I don't know if I'm more scared of the monsters or of Sir Thomas seeing me be scared of the monsters. I can only vaguely see him behind us. Why is he so far away?

So you will die first.

106

Stop!

Honestly, I was kind of hoping he'd punch or karate chop some people. But I guess that's illegal.

Through each room, I jump and yell and claw at McGruff until we finally open a door and see daylight.

Thank goodness that's over.

Or is it?

I scream as something touches my back from behind. Quickly turning I see Sir Thomas standing there with his wife on his arm.

Jen looks concerned. From the corner of my eye, I see McGruff staring at me. Sir Thomas narrows his eyes.

Throwing my head back, I burst into laughter. McGruff and Jen do the same. I swear I see the corner of Sir Thomas' mouth curve up.

"Next up," Sir Thomas states.

Next? We have to do more?

We do whatever Sir Thomas tells us to do.

Immediately, Sir Thomas spins around and walks away. Jen quickly follows. McGruff grabs my arm and tugs me forward with him. We all form another single file line.

I'm in the army now. Sir Thomas' army.

Is that a good thing?

I'm not sure yet.

Will you end up like McGruff? Needing to control everything?

Oh, God. I hope not. I literally cannot control a thing.

CHAPTER EIGHT

"What's that face for?" Walter asks. He is sitting on the couch next to me.

"Ugh, I have a meeting," I respond and scowl at the laptop on my lap.

"A bad one?"

"It's not horrible. I probably won't have to talk much, but Jack is in it."

"Oh, he's the mean guy?"

"He's the one."

"I can leave so you can meet."

"No, don't go. It will probably be short."

Walter rests against the couch and says, "All right, but you just tell me if I'm a bother."

"You're never a bother, Walter."

I inhale and hit the join meeting button. The cyber conference room opens. I am the only one here.

Ah, well. No one's probably in the physical conference room yet. Jack is most likely speed walking down the aisles to get there. Then, someone has to figure out how to turn on the computer and pull up the meeting invite. That's usually my job when Raj or some offshore employee is waiting patiently alone in cyberspace.

"Is this the meeting?" Walter whispers.

"No. Well, yes. I am the only one here. I am waiting for the people in the office to log on."

"They're all together?"

"Yeah. They will all meet in person in the conference room and then just log into the online meeting from there. They'll all be sitting around the table staring at the phone."

"Wouldn't you rather be in the conference room with them?"

"Oh, heck no."

Walter laughs. "I like our Monday mornings."

"So do I," I say as I sip my coffee and stare at my lone name on the meeting's participants list.

"Did I tell you that Josh is coming back?"

What? So soon? He was just here a few months ago.

"No, you didn't."

"He's coming in a couple of weeks. He's going to take me back to New York City with him for Thanksgiving. I will stay there with him for a couple of weeks."

No. Nope. This is just Josh's ploy to get Walter to move to New York to be closer to him.

It's going to work. Walter will probably love being around his son and granddaughter.

Shut up.

"So, I was thinking," he continues, "that while Josh is here, we can have one of those...what do you kids call it? When you have Thanksgiving with people that aren't your family? Your friends?"

"Oh! Friendsgiving."

"Yes. I thought we could have one of those at my apartment with Josh and Sally. And you could bring Nate."

"Yes, I would love that."

"Okay, great. I haven't gotten far into the plan, so I will tell you when and what to bring soon."

"Sounds good. Will Julia be coming?"

"No. Josh thought that since we'd just be coming right back, it would be best if she stayed home."

"I was hoping I'd get to meet that granddaughter of yours."

"I know. You'll meet her eventually."

"I'm glad you invited Sally. I'm sure she makes a killer Thanksgiving meal."

"I'm banking on it," he says and winks.

Maybe McGruff can make our dishes to bring.

No, you can make one. Or at least try to.

I can bring the wine.

Just make sure it's up to Josh's standards. He's a wine connoisseur.

"Are people supposed to be talking in this meeting of yours?" Walter asks.

Oh, that's right. I'm in a meeting. Or I'm supposed to be, anyway, but no one else has logged into the virtual meeting. They must not have been able to get the computer in the room working.

No, they just forgot about you.

That's probably the best case scenario. I didn't skip it, so Carl can't be mad at me. I was here in cyberspace waiting for the soft and distant voices of my coworkers to mumble through my computer.

I was stood up.

"It looks like they forgot about me, Walter."

"That's not right."

No one even messaged me. They legitimately forgot I was supposed to be there. I know they don't really need me or even notice me, but geez, this neglect kind of hurts.

"It's actually fine. I didn't want to go to the meeting anyway," I say as I hit the leave meeting button.

You did it. You achieved invisibility.

"I still think it's rude," he replies.

Yes. But I am glad I don't have to deal with Jack right now. I'm not upset.

You are a little.

"It's okay. Now I get to spend more time with you."

"Deal. But I am leaving before your next meeting."

Which unfortunately is in less than twenty minutes. Taking a sip of coffee, I leisurely check my email as the envelope has popped up in the bar to announce a new arrival.

"Ahhh!" I yell, spilling coffee down the front of my chest.

Walter grabs my elbow. "Are you okay?"

"No!"

"Did the coffee burn you?"

"No! It's worse," I say, close my laptop, place it on the coffee table, and lean back against the couch.

"What is it?"

"It's a meeting with my new VP."

"That's bad?"

"She said she'd be setting up meetings to talk to the department and most would be group meetings. Nick already got his invite, and he is in a group."

"And?"

"And I'm not! It's just me! Alone! With her!"

"I see. Well, the way I look at it, is that she wants to talk to you personally. That is a good thing."

He's right.

Shut up. This is horrible.

No, it's not. She wants to speak with you alone. She thinks you are worthy of an individual meeting.

Yeah, alone!

You will be fine. She is not Bob. She seems really nice. Plus, you made Bob laugh, remember?

One time!

"Gemma?"

"Yeah. I know. I am just freaking out about it."

"Trust me. You'll do fine," he says and squeezes my elbow. "But it is almost time for your next meeting. I must be off."

Walter finishes his coffee, and I walk him to the door. Sitting back down, I hit the join meeting button.

Please forget about me. Please forget about me, again. I can't deal with a meeting right now.

Hey, you were hurt that they forgot about you earlier.

I'm over it. I'd rather be forgotten than actually have to participate in meetings.

But alas, Nick's name appears in the participants list, and I hear him announce, "We're here! I wouldn't forget about you, Gemma. Just had some computer issues."

"I knew you'd show up."

I didn't want you to, but I knew you would.

"All right," I vaguely hear from Carl, who is probably sitting too far from the phone for me to properly hear him.

I hear some more muffled voices as the spreadsheet is pulled up in the virtual meeting and appears on my computer screen.

"Okay!"

I flinch at the sound. Oh, that was definitely Jack. I am so thankful that I am not sitting in that conference room right now.

If you were, you'd at least be able to hear and understand what everyone is saying.

Overrated. If Carl knew I couldn't hear or understand anything that happened in these meetings, he would take away my precious work from home days, and I couldn't survive that.

You don't know that he'd take them away. Maybe he would just speak louder.

I can't risk it.

There are more muffled voices, and the spreadsheet on the screen scrolls down a few lines.

Jumbled words. Jumbled words.

"Right, Gemma?" Crystal clear. Carl must have leaned over the phone before he spoke.

You have to tell him you didn't hear anything.

No. I can do this. The cursor is on the row for the address system change. He is asking if I'm all set.

What if you're wrong?

"Right, Carl."

Got to roll the dice once in a while.

You're just going to ask Nick.

Of course, I am. That's how I get through all of my meetings. Heaven knows I can't pay attention even when I *can* hear what's going on.

Shouldn't you at least pay attention to the spreadsheet on your screen?

I suppose.

Good. What line are they on?

Oh heck, I have no clue. I'll check in with Nick after.

Any more meetings after this one?

I pull up my calendar. A few. None with Jack.

Phew.

Oh, and don't forget you have your appointment with Stacey after work.

Super. I love talking about my feelings.

Since I have been feeling a little better, I have graduated to seeing Stacey every other week instead of every week.

That's not really graduating.

Promoted? Demoted?

Anyway, she thinks I'm not in need of her service every week anymore. I think that's progress.

As I sit in the small waiting room, bloodying my cuticles, a man quietly walks in through the door, closes it, and chooses a seat against the adjacent wall.

I hate being in the room with only one other person. Do I smile? Do I say hi? I'd much rather be alone.

And it appears he would too, because he doesn't even look at me. He just pulls out his phone and starts scrolling.

"Gemma?"

I look up and see Stacey waiting for me. She is only about five feet two inches and has her blonde hair cut into a pixie. I follow her down the hall and into a door on the right. Taking my respective seat, I place my purse onto the seat next to me as Stacey sits across the room. The room is small, so across the room is only a few feet. Her seat is slightly higher than mine, giving her a more authoritative presence over little old me.

"How have you been?" she starts.

"I've been good."

I never know whether asking her how she has been is appropriate or not, so I never do. And I also never know how much to lead off with in this first greeting, so I only say that I am good. I wonder if people use that opening as a way to just jump into their feelings? Do people just start gabbing away?

"Is there anything new?" she asks.

"Yes."

You're going to expound on that, right?

"Bob, my VP," I continue, "is retiring. And his replacement seems really nice. I have a meeting scheduled with her next week."

"Oh, how do you feel about Bob retiring?"

"I don't want to sound mean, but I'm kind of happy about it. That guy intimidates me."

"When is his last day?"

"It was last week."

"Wow. That was fast."

"Yeah. I guess they didn't announce it to us peons until they had everything in place with his replacement."

"What do you think of his replacement? Have you spoken to her yet?"

"I haven't spoken to her personally, but she did speak to the department. She seems really intelligent. Her big new idea is Inclusion and Diversity."

"That sounds promising. Are you nervous about meeting with her?"

"Yes. She obviously makes me anxious, but I have a feeling I won't be as anxious as when I had to meet with Bob."

"Why do you think that is?"

"She has a warmer personality. She seems more human, if that makes sense."

"Yes, it does."

"Plus, with the Inclusion and Diversity platform, I feel like she'll be more understanding."

"She probably will. Do you know what you'll be talking about in your meeting with her? Is it just the two of you?"

I sigh. "Yes, just the two of us. I don't know if that makes it more or less stressful. And there is no real topic. She basically wants to meet with everyone and chat."

"How do you feel about that?"

"Horrible. I can't chat to save my life."

Stacey smiles. "You're chatting now."

"This is different."

"You should prepare things you want to discuss with her. That will make it less stressful. You can make talking points to rehearse. This will also help to keep the conversation moving so there are no silent moments."

"Yeah, I can try to think of some."

"May I suggest that you talk to her about working from home and your anxiety?"

"What about it?"

"You said she's a proponent of Inclusion and Diversity. If you were looking to have more days at home or more flexibility, then I would bring it up to her."

"Actually tell her about my anxiety?"

"You shouldn't be embarrassed by it, Gemma. If your employers knew more about it, then they would be more willing to help you and say yes to your requests, such as more days working at home."

She makes a good point. But will I have the guts to talk to Jaqueline about it? Probably not.

"Do you not want more days at home?"

"Of course, I do. I would love to work from home full time again."

"There's only one way to make that happen. You have to advocate for yourself. I know you don't like doing that, but sometimes you have to if you want to get what you want. And this new VP seems like the exact right person to ask."

"You don't think Carl will get mad if I go over his head?"

"No. She called the meeting with you, and she is asking for your opinions. Carl can't get mad about that."

"No, I guess that's true."

You need to talk to her about working from home. This is your one chance. You had the courage to ask Carl, and he said yes.

But only for two days a week. It wasn't every day.

"Good. Think about it. If that's what you really want, then I think you should bring it up to her. The worst she can say is no."

And then I will obsess about it for the rest of my life.

"I will. I just need to figure out what to say."

And then rehearse it over and over until you meet with her and you still forget what you want to say.

"Good. Anything else new?"

"I went to Foxwoods with Brittany for a conference. A management conference."

"Why the tone in your voice?"

"I don't know why Carl thinks I could be management. He wants me on a project manager track."

"And you don't want to be?"

"Do you think I could be management?"

"I think you could do anything you put your mind to."

Aww, shucks.

"Well, maybe, but I don't think I'm cut out for it. I hate leading meetings, and I'm bad at it."

"Then we both know what you have to do."

Quit?

"I know. Talk to Carl."

"Yes. How was the conference?"

"It was good. I actually had a lot of fun with Brittany and Ed."

"Tell me about Ed."

"He is thirty years old, but acts like he's in his teens. He's really outgoing and easy to talk to."

"He pulls you out of your shell a little."

"You can say that," I say and smile.

"What are you thinking?"

"He got us tickets to a dance club and we all went and danced together. I did get too drunk and had to leave before them."

"Sounds like you got out of your comfort zone."

"Did I ever. We even went ziplining."

"Wow, Gemma. Good for you."

"Thank you. I was feeling pretty good, but Nate's been getting mad at me for drinking so much, especially while taking Celexa."

Stacey nods. "Yeah, it's not recommended to drink while taking your medication."

"I know. But I need to drink to relax in social situations. I drank at Foxwoods and again at Bob's retirement party. And yes, I had a little too much."

"It sounds like Nate is worried."

"I'm not drinking more than I did before."

"No, but you react differently now. I think you should take that into consideration. The medication makes the effect of alcohol worse. Nate cares about you. Also, I think it would be a good idea for you to see if your medication is working instead of pre-emptively self-medicating with alcohol. You may not need to anymore."

Oh. Right.

"Yeah, maybe."

Very noncommittal.

"How is everything else with Nate? Any problems lately?"

"Nothing with Nate. His parents came into town this weekend. It was Nate's birthday, but he hadn't told me it was his birthday. Not that I remembered. We all went to Salem to walk around. I had a panic attack in the crowds, and he was really helpful and understanding. His mom is really nice. His dad...I don't know if you remember me talking about him, but he's retired from the military and is very strict and stern and is the cause of Nate's anxiety...or control issues."

"I do remember you saying that. How was it being out with them?"

"His mom is great. But his dad makes me uncomfortable."

"How so?"

"He brings out my anxiety, but at the same time I kind of like him."

"I see."

"Yeah. It makes me wonder if Nate and I stay together, how I will be able to handle him as my father-in-law."

"Do you think you'd end your relationship with Nate because of his dad?"

"Oh, no. I just...I am sure it will get better if I see him more often. He wasn't as bad as I thought."

Why did you have to bring this up? You like Sir Thomas, don't you?

Yes, but he does make me extremely anxious. But at the same time, I have no doubt it will get better the more I see him.

You just wanted to change the subject from your drinking.

"Have you talked to Nate about your feelings about his dad?"

"No."

She's going to tell you to talk to him. That's going to be your homework this week.

"Do you think it would be beneficial to have Nate come here with you for your next appointment, and we can all talk about his father and even your drinking?"

"What?"

I didn't see that coming. I could have sworn it was going to be a take home assignment.

Look what you did. You brought up something you're not really worried about and now you have to bring Nate in with you to talk about it.

"Have him come in with you. The three of us can talk."

I don't like this idea.

"I can see you're not loving the thought, so just think about it. If you want to bring him, then just bring him along next time. If not, then you should talk to him about your feelings."

Gross. Talk about my feelings?

That's what you've been doing for the past hour. And you do it every time you're here with Stacey.

I've gotten pretty good at it. I barely cringe when she asks, "How does that make you feel?"

And how does that make you feel?

Oh, shut up.

CHAPTER NINE

I can feel my anxiety starting in my stomach and boiling up my body like a geyser, no a volcano, ready to burst and destroy everything in its path. My breath quickens, followed by my heartbeat.

You are going to be fine. You are going to be fine. Just breathe. In and out.

I take a deep breath and hold it for four seconds before exhaling.

You can do this. You are a warrior princess.

In and out. In and out.

I can still feel my heart racing. Why do deep breaths never calm me down fully? Do breathing exercises work for other people, or is it just a myth?

It's probably just you. Your anxiety is an unstoppable beast.

No. I need to think positively. My medication has been helping. I need to do my part and not give in to the unrelenting monster trying to break its way out of my skull and ribcage simultaneously. I must stop it.

How? It's unstoppable.

Shut up! I will slow it down then.

Taking another deep breath, I lower my chin to my chest and close my eyes.

Man, I should've called out sick today.

She would have rescheduled, and you would have looked like a bad employee.

Putting two fingers on my neck, I feel my pulse, still racing, but not as fast.

You're doing it! You are calming down.

Let's not get too excited here. I still need to survive the meeting.

And it's time. Taking one more giant breath, I lock my computer, stand up, and walk towards the new VP's corner office. What if the door is closed? Do I knock? What if the door is open? Do I knock?

As I approach, I can see that the door is open. When I get to the doorway, Jaqueline looks up and smiles. She was waiting for me. Bob would have never done that. He would have been working and would have been annoyed that I interrupted him for a meeting that he himself set up.

"Gemma, please come in," she says as she gets up from her chair and motions towards the table on the other side of the room.

As I sit, she closes the door to her office and then sits across from me.

"Thank you for coming," she says.

Did I have a choice?

Shut up. She's being nice. Bob never would have thanked you.

She looks at me with kind brown eyes, the opposite of Bob's icy blues.

"I just want to start by saying that I've heard from multiple people that you are an all-star, Gemma. You are highly respected. I've been looking forward to meeting with you."

Well, shucks. How should I respond to compliments? I never know.

"Thank you," I murmur.

"How is everything work-wise?"

"It's good."

Way to really expand on that, Gemma. She's looking for a conversation here.

"Do you feel like you don't have enough work? Or you have too much work?"

Do I tell her the truth?

Yes? Well, maybe not. Maybe a half-truth.

"Honestly, at times I feel like it's maybe leaning towards too much, but I always get it done."

"I know you do. But I don't want anyone to get burnt out."

She is the complete opposite of Bob.

"Tell me a little about yourself."

Ah, shit. I hate that statement. I never know what to say. There is nothing interesting in my life.

"I've worked here for a little over five years. I graduated from BU."

"Do you live in the city?"

"Yes, I have an apartment a few blocks away."

"Siblings?"

"I have an older brother. He lives in Maine with my parents."

"Oh, you're originally from Maine?"

"Yes."

"What part?"

"It's a town named Oxford. It's maybe a three hour drive from here."

"I love Maine, especially in the summer."

"Yeah, the winters can be tough."

"I bet. You moved down here for school, then?"

"Yes, I really love the city."

"I do, too."

What is happening here?

She is trying to put you at ease.

Well, it's working. She's so easy to talk to. It's so comfortable. She's so welcoming. It's weird. I don't like being put at ease.

Gemma! What are you doing? You are now having anxiety about being comfortable. You need to stop.

"Carl tells me he has started putting you into more of a project manager role."

"Yes, he has."

"How are you liking it?"

What do I tell her? The truth? Half-truth again?

"You can be honest," she says.

Honest? Okay, I'll try that.

"I'm not really sure that it is for me."

"I see. Why do you think that?"

Tell her about your anxiety.

No, she's not Stacey.

Well, right now she feels like Stacey.

I can't tell her about it.

Why not? She wants to know your opinion, and there's never going to be another chance like this. She seems like she'll understand.

I don't want people to know.

Why not?

I don't know. It's a weakness.

No, it's not. And you know that.

To some people it is.

Maybe not to her. Give her a chance.

"I don't think it's a good fit for me."

"Everything that I hear about you makes me believe you are up to the task."

This is it. You have to tell her. It's the perfect opportunity. She will understand.

"You don't want to be a manager?" she asks. "It's not for everyone. Some people don't want to have to manage other people. They don't always cooperate." She smiles.

Tell her damn it!

"Well, that's part of it. You see I have…"

Yes! You can do it! You have to!

"I have…I have an anxiety disorder and having to lead meetings, and actually meetings in general, give me a lot of anxiety."

You did it! You told her!

Yeah, but now what?

"I see," she says and scratches her chin.

Oh, no. I shouldn't have told her. Now I'm embarrassed.

"Well, as you know," she says, "I am a proponent of inclusion and diversity, and I think that falls under the umbrella. I want everyone to feel comfortable here, Gemma. And if you feel that being a project manager is not for you, then I respect that."

Phew.

"Thank you."

"May I ask if your anxiety is why you work from home two days a week?"

Oh my God. That's a perfect segue. You have to ask about doing it full time now.

Slow down! I can barely breathe.

I take a deep breath.

"Yes. While the building was closed, I found that my anxiety level was a lot lower, and I could function better at my job and in meetings."

"May I ask why that is? I'm only curious because I don't have that kind of anxiety myself, so I'd like to understand it more. Understand you more."

"I guess it's that I don't have to physically be there. It's not as bad."

"It's the separation?"

"Yes."

"Okay. Would you prefer to work from home full time, or were two days all you asked for?"

Holy shit. This is going better than I thought it would. I don't have to bring any of this up. She's doing it herself.

"Well, ideally full time would be what I'd like, but Carl and Bob said I could have two days, so I was happy they even said that."

"I see. As a business analyst, you do have a lot of responsibilities that require speaking to a lot of other people and departments, to gather requirements and such, so I'm not sure one hundred percent remote work is doable."

Well, shit. My chest deflates.

"Have you heard of an ADA accommodation, Gemma?"

A what now?

"No, I haven't."

She reaches up, gently scratches behind her ear, and says, "ADA stands for Americans with Disabilities Act…"

Wait, what? Disabilities?

She continues, "and I believe anxiety is a covered disability."

Again, with the D word.

"The act requires that companies accommodate employees with disabilities who make a request, such as working from home full-time, even though their company does not usually allow it."

Hold on.

"You can put in a request with HR to work from home full-time. They may need a note from your doctor, but you can get the ball rolling with HR today if you'd like."

I'm not sure how to respond. I am not sure how I feel about this conversation. She is saying I have a disability. But she is also saying I can work from home full-time.

"Do you have any questions about that, Gemma?"

I can feel my blood boiling up throughout my body.

Calm down. This is the same person you were talking to, and you were calm. What are you doing getting anxious now?

She called me disabled.

Gemma, there is nothing wrong with having a disability.

I know! But I don't have one!

Are you sure?

"Gemma?"

"I can ask HR to work from home?"

"Yes, you'd have to phrase it as an ADA accommodation, but yes. Do you have a doctor or physician that could write you a letter if necessary?"

I have Janet my medication prescriber. And Stacey my therapist.

"Yes."

"Okay, great."

What am I feeling right now?

Confusion. Hurt. Shame. Happiness.

"I didn't mean to upset you, Gemma. I just wanted you to have all of the facts. You are a valuable employee, and I just want to make you comfortable here, even if that means not working *here*," she says and smiles. "I see I've given you some things to think about, but know that my door is always open to you, and I mean that."

"Thank you," I murmur.

Get up. Get up, Gemma. You have to leave now. I know you are dumbfounded, but you have to leave.

And I do.

McGruff has already texted when I get back to my desk and sit down.

"How'd it go?" he asks.

I still don't know.

"Interesting," I respond.

"How so? Do tell!"

"I will tell you after work."

"Okay."

What do I tell him, though?

You can think about that later. Right now, you have to think about your meeting with Jack. Remember you are the leader.

Great. There is no way that Jack is walking out of the meeting today. No way. You aren't that lucky. He will stay in there and torture you.

I know. I know he will, but at least I have the other three guys, right? They will help me deal with him, won't they?

Girl, they wanted to vote him out last week, and you didn't. They will not be happy when he shows up today.

Well, I won't be happy either. But I can't think of a way to get rid of him.

You know, you should really move these meetings to Monday when you aren't in the office.

Brilliant idea. But I doubt Carl would go for it.

Sitting down at the conference room table, I look up as Jack grunts through the door.

Damn it. Why'd he have to show up first? He's never on time to meetings.

"Morning, Jack," I say.

"Yep," he mumbles as he sits.

Oh, goodie. He's in a great mood today.

Joe arrives next. He looks at Jack and then looks at me disapprovingly.

I couldn't figure out how to exclude him, and no one gave me any ideas, either.

"Morning," Joe greets us.

I smile and Jack grunts. Joe gives me another look, and I frown in response.

Nick is next to walk through the door. He also looks at Jack and then glares at me before sitting in the chair next to mine.

"Morning, Joe," he says, purposefully leaving me out.

Joe smiles, and I shake my head. I can see the corner of Nick's mouth turn upward and immediately fall as he tries to not grin. Jack is oblivious.

Ed is the last to arrive. He looks at Jack, audibly exhales, glances at me with an annoyed look, and closes the door before sitting next to Jack. Ed crosses his arms over his chest and sighs.

Shaking my head, I pull up the requirements spreadsheet on the computer screen.

"I'm so disappointed in you, Gemma," Ed finally says.

"Me too," Nick adds.

"Same here," Joe chimes in.

"What did she do now?" Jack asks.

Now? What did I do *now*? What have I ever done to you, Jack, besides refrain from punching you in the face every single day of my life?

"Oh," Ed answers, "We asked her to do one thing for us, and she didn't. One *measly* thing. And she didn't come through."

The grins on Joe's and Nick's faces drop when Jack responds, "Typical Gemma."

What the hell, buddy? You are the bane of my existence. If I believed in voodoo dolls, I would have a whole room full of you that I could torture.

Dark, Gemma. That's dark.

He deserves it! Look at his smug ass face. I want to punch it.

"Hey!" Ed shouts. "That's not typical Gemma at all. She's ten times the worker than most of these fools in this company."

Aww, he does like me.

"Yeah, Jack," Nick adds. "We were just joking with her. We weren't serious."

That's right. Have to stand up for your fellow pack members because God knows I won't stand up for myself, especially to Jack.

"I was kidding, too," Jack replies.

"No, you weren't," Joe says. "That was just mean."

They are all defending me to Jack. This is so sweet, but I need to take control of this God forsaken meeting. Would Carl let this happen? No. Would Carl need people to defend him? No. Would Carl just say okay let's table this and move on? Yes. Will I do that? No. I am so bad at leading meetings. I will never be a project manager.

You can do this, just say something. You are a God damn warrior princess. You can take control of this meeting. Besides, it's getting awkward.

"Okay, let's just move on," I say.

Look at you! Carl would be proud.

Jack huffs and says, "Finally."

I will finally your ass.

128

What does that even mean?

I don't know. I am angry and hurt and anxious, and I don't know what to do or say. I just want to get up and walk out. I can feel my eyes start to well.

Don't! Just breathe. You don't want to have a panic attack now, do you?

I take a deep breath in and slowly exhale as Joe reaches across the table and slides the keyboard and mouse from in front of me and places them in front of him.

"Okay," Joe says, "Let's go through the requirements."

"I'll start," Ed responds.

Oh, my God. I love these guys. Not only will they defend me, but they will also lead this meeting themselves, even though I know they don't even want to be here.

Joe goes through the spreadsheet, and the other three respond and add steps as necessary while my heartbeat slowly returns to its normal pace. My head feels more grounded, and my hands no longer shake.

You're fine. Look at you.

Sure, I'm fine now. But I failed once again at being a manager. There's no way I can actually do this job.

You don't have to. Remember that. If you don't get the data warehouse developer job, you still don't have to become a project manager. You don't want to, and you need to tell that to Carl.

What data warehouse developer job? It's not even posted yet. No one has even mentioned that Larry has quit.

It will. Be patient.

"All right. That's a wrap for today," Joe says.

I mouth the words "thank you," and Joe nods. As I stand up, Nick touches my elbow.

"Pack lunch?" he asks.

I nod.

"I'll message Brit."

Brit? She's Brit now?

But he doesn't have to. Brittany is waiting at my desk as Nick and I walk back from our meeting. When she sees me, her eyes light up, she smiles, and claps her hands together.

"It's up!" she says when I am back at my cubicle.

Nick stops next to Brittany and asks, "What's up?"

Brittany smiles. "Oh, nothing much."

"Funny," he says, walks to his own desk, and sits down.

Turning my head to look down my cubicle row, I notice Carl is not at his desk. My heart starts to pound. Why am I nervous? This is stupid. Nothing has even happened yet. I've barely thought about anything happening.

"When are you going to do it?" Brittany asks excitedly.

Brittany's excitement means that the job posting for Larry's position was just posted. This is what I've been waiting for, so why am I now hesitant to apply?

That's just you being you. You know you want to apply, so just do it.

"Well," I respond. "I have to get Carl's permission before I apply for it. It's company policy that you have to notify your current manager before you apply for another internal position."

"When are you going to ask Carl?" she follows up with.

I need to calm down. Why is Brittany pressuring me like this?

She's not. She is just excited for you. She knows you really want the job.

"I don't know. I'll set up a meeting with him."

"For today?"

"If there is room on his calendar."

"Geez, Brit," Nick says, appearing at Brittany's side again. "Give Gemma some breathing room here. She just got out of a crappy meeting with Jack. She needs some time to process. I'm sure she will do whatever it is you want her to do. Right, Gemma?"

I exhale. "Right."

"See," Nick says. "Anyway, you threw me off with your intensity, I forgot to tell you that we have decided that we are doing a pack lunch today. You in?" he asks Brittany.

"I'm always in for a pack lunch."

"Good," Nick replies. "We'll meet back here at noon. Now let's break."

Nick and Brittany turn in opposite directions and walk away. I hear Nick settle down in his cube next to mine as I do the same.

This is it, Gemma. It's go time. This is what you've been waiting for. There's no time like the present. Set up a meeting with Carl. Once that's done, then you can start working on the application.

Pulling up a new meeting request, I scan Carl's schedule for an open time slot today. He is free at 4:30. The last meeting of the day. Perfect. I can meet with him and then run out of the building.

What should I call the meeting? I type in the name, using the same title that Carl uses when he wants to randomly meet with me. "Quick Meeting." I always think I'm going to get fired in those quick meetings, but I never do. Maybe Carl will think I'm quitting. It is the last meeting of the day. Huh! The tables have turned. It's his turn to be worried about what the meeting will be about.

You are kind of quitting. Quitting his team, at least.

Oh, right. It *is* bad news for him.

A few minutes later, he walks briskly by my desk, and returns to his own. I wait patiently for him to accept my invite.

Why am I holding my breath? He's obviously going to accept it. Why am I so anxious?

I exhale when I see his acceptance in my inbox. Now to worry about what I'm going to say to him. He won't be mad, right? No, he can't be. Probably.

Stop it. He won't be mad at you. The worst that will happen will that he'll be disappointed in you, like a father would.

Before I know it, Brittany is returning to my desk to head out to lunch. She stops in front of me, puts her forearms on the front of my cube, leans over, and quietly asks, "So?"

"Stop talking about me," Nick says from his desk through the partition. "You know I hate when you whisper about me while I'm sitting right here."

Brittany grins. I ignore him and say quietly back to Brittany, "I set up a meeting with Carl at 4:30 today."

Her eyes open wide and a big smile lights up her face.

Nick gets up from his desk, stands next to Brittany, and crosses his arms over his chest.

"Why am I not included in any of this pack business today?"

"Who says it's pack business?" I ask.

"Yeah," Brittany replies. "We could be talking about lady business."

"Ew," Nick responds.

"That's right, ew," I say.

"No, we were saying," Brittany replies, puts her hand to her mouth, and whispers in Nick's ear.

Nick looks at me, furrows his brow, and then rolls his eyes.

"I don't know what she said to you," I say. "But I don't think it's true."

Nick shakes his head. "Oh, it was nonsense."

Brittany smirks and says, "Let's skedaddle."

"Where to?" Nick asks and looks at me.

"Sally's? I could go for some mac and cheese right now," I respond.

"Yes!" Brittany answers. "Mac and cheese times two."

"Make that times three," Nick adds.

We make our way out into the chilly autumn air and down a few blocks to Sally's. To my disappointment, Walter is not there.

"Hey, hons," Sally greets us.

132

Before Sally can say anything else, Nick says, "Mac and cheese all around, please Sally."

Sally smiles. "You got it."

Within a minute, we are sitting at a table with our respective plates of pasta.

"What did you think of Jaqueline?" Nick asks me. "I had my round table last week."

"You had a round table?" Brittany asks, presumably because I told her I was meeting with her alone.

And by told, you mean freaked out to her.

Yes.

"Yeah. A few of us in the department where there. What did you have?" he asks me.

"I had a one-on-one with her."

"All by yourself?" Nick asks.

"Just me and her."

Brittany and Nick look at each other and then back at me.

"How'd that go?" Nick asks.

Good question. What do I say? Half-truth?

"It wasn't that bad, actually. She's very easy to talk to. How was your meeting?"

"It was good," Nick answers. "She tried to get to know us a little. I like her."

"Yeah, same. So do I. But she was saying how happy she was that I am good at being a BA, so now I feel weird for immediately applying for Larry's job."

Surprised, Nick asks, "You are?"

"Yeah, I thought Brittany would have told you."

"What? You knew?" he asks Brittany.

"Maybe…" Brittany responds quietly.

"Why didn't you tell me?"

"I thought Gemma would have told you, and when I realized you didn't know, I didn't want to over step."

"This is what you two were talking about earlier?"

"Yeah," I say.

"I am so the third wheel in this pack," Nick says and sighs.

Actually, I am pretty sure I am. Or I am about to be, anyway. Brittany and Nick seem to be getting closer.

"I'm sorry," Brittany apologizes.

We sit in silence as we finish our lunch. Nick and Brittany appear to be making eyes at each other. Oh, my God. I *am* the third wheel. Who else can join our pack? Ed? Do new members need to be voted in? How does that work? Should I nominate him?

Do you really want Ed in your pack?

Maybe, if it means that I don't have to sit here awkwardly alone while Brittany and Nick flirt with each other. Maybe McGruff can be a member? Do members have to work at KPM? Wait, didn't they already nominate him at Bob's retirement party? Why didn't we invite him to lunch today?

"Do you forgive me?" Brittany asks shyly and bats her eyes.

Oh, my God. Gross. I need to leave.

"I will always forgive you," Nick responds.

"Good," Brittany replies, and they continue to silently stare into each other's eyes.

No! I can't be here. Can I quietly leave without saying anything? They probably won't even notice.

I look over at Sally, who raises her eyebrows twice and smiles. Taking that as an invitation, I get up with my plate, hand it to Sally, and whisper, "Ugh."

She smiles. "Oh, come on," she says. "You and Nate were just as bad. Only Brittany isn't running away from him."

Burn. Why do people have to throw that in my face? It's not like I wanted to do that. I would much rather be a normal human being like Brittany.

I turn to peek at the table, and they are whispering and smiling at each other. They didn't even notice I had left. Looking back at Sally, I cringe.

"They should get a room, huh?" Sally says.

I nod and frown.

"What's the face for?" she asks.

"I feel like I'm losing my pack. We just got our rhythm. We were a good little coworker friend group."

"Don't worry, honey. You will be again. This is just new. Give it time."

Sure, but what will I do until it's normal again?

Gemma, it's fine. You're the one that is making this weird. They will still be your pack.

I sigh and look back at them. Do I leave without them? Do I interrupt? What's the protocol here? Turning back, I shrug at Sally.

"Will I see you at Walter's Friendsgiving?" Sally asks me.

"Yep. I'll be there with Nate."

"Oh, good. I was hoping he'd go."

"What are you making?"

"I'm not sure yet. Maybe a couple of things. What about you?"

"I'm not sure, either."

Maybe buying a couple things.

Sally smiles. "Wine is always appreciated."

Brittany and Nick come over and hand Sally their plates.

"Ready to go back?" Brittany asks.

I have never been so ready to go back to the office in all my life.

"Yep," I respond.

"Bye," Sally says as Brittany and Nick walk out the door, leaving me to trail after.

I wave at Sally, and she waves back.

So much for these two remembering that I am here. I put my hands on my hips and look down as I walk.

"Gemma!" Brittany says as she grabs my elbow and loops her arm around mine.

Okay, maybe they do remember me.

We walk in a row until we enter the building and ride up the elevator.

"Good luck in your meeting," Brittany whispers as she passes my desk to go back to her own.

Oh, yeah. That. It's my only meeting this afternoon, so the rest of my day is wide open for obsessing and dreading.

Seriously? It's going to be fine. It's just Carl. Tell him you want to apply. That's all you have to do. It will be a two minute meeting. Don't stress. Clear your mind of it.

But I don't. I pick at my cuticles, tap my pen, and avoid panic attacks all afternoon until it's time to meet with Carl. He's not at his desk when I get up and walk to the conference room, which means he's in another meeting and will most likely be late. That gives me time to sit alone in the room and stress some more until he finally shows up, and then I'll be a hot mess.

Gemma! Pull it together. You are better than this.

Yes, I am better than this. I am a God damn warrior princess who can absolutely muster the courage to tell Carl that I don't want to work for him anymore.

Maybe don't word it like that.

"Gemma," Carl says as he closes the door behind him.

My head snaps up, and I watch him sit directly across from me. He smiles, places his pad of paper onto the desk, and waits. And waits.

Gemma, this is your meeting. You have to talk. Tell him why he is here.

"So," I say hesitantly. "I just wanted to…I need your…I would like to apply for the data warehouse developer position, and I need your approval. Larry's job."

Rough start, but you pulled through.

Carl crosses his arms over his chest and says, "I see."

136

Oh, boy. He's going to say no.

He can't say no, can he?

What's the point of having to ask, if he can't say no? He's got to have the option.

"This is what you want?"

"Yes."

"Does this have anything to do with me pushing you towards the project manager track?"

Does it? Yes. But it was only the catalyst. I would have wanted to apply for this job even if Carl didn't want me to be a project manager.

"Because, you don't have to be a PM," Carl continues. "If you just want to stay a BA, that is perfectly fine. I just wanted to give you the opportunity for career advancement, since you are a great employee. But if you don't want that, then no hard feelings. You can stay a BA as long as you would like. That's fine."

Oh, boy. This is worse than him saying no. He wants me to stay.

Of course, he does. You're awesome. He told you that you were one of his best employees, remember? And now you just want to leave him high and dry. Look at him. He's sad.

Yeah, and now I have to tell him again that I want to leave even though he's trying to make me happy so that I will stay. Damn it. Why can't I be assertive? I just need to confirm that yes, I want to apply and not care about his feelings at all. Care about my own feelings for once. Do it. Tell him. Now.

"I know," I respond. "It's not just the PM track. I'd want to apply either way. I think I'd really like the job and that I'm suited for it better than this one."

"I see," he says again. "Well, if that's what you really want, then of course, you can apply. I'd hate to see you leave, but I'm not going to stand in your way. And, if by some chance, you don't get the job, I want you to be honest about being a PM or if you want to stay a BA. But that's a future conversation if it comes to it."

"Thanks, Carl. I appreciate it."

"Is there anything else you want to talk about?"

"That was it."

"Okay, well, good luck, Gemma," he says, gets up, pushes in his chair, and leaves the conference room.

Still sitting, I exhale deeply. That's over with. Now, all I have to do is apply, interview, wait for the verdict, and dread every step of the way, all the while maintaining my current workload and meeting schedule without completely imploding from the pressure. No biggie.

You're so dramatic. Just go back to your desk and wait out the next twenty minutes so that you can leave for the day.

As I exit the elevator on the way out, McGruff immediately grabs my arm.

"Were you just waiting by the elevator for me?" I ask.

"Yes! You've made me wait all day to hear about your day."

"Oh my, there's so much to tell."

"Well, then get started."

CHAPTER TEN

Don't you think that you should confirm?

Liz and I never confirm plans if we're going.

You haven't talked to her in a while, and you haven't been out to Flannery's on a Saturday in a few weeks.

I take out my phone and send, "We still on?"

She immediately texts back, "Oh, you're going to come?"

Damn.

"I was planning to, but if you don't want to, I won't."

"Fine."

"So, you'll be there?"

"Yes."

I am not sure I even want to go now. She doesn't seem like she wants to see me.

She said she'd be there.

Yeah, but she didn't seem happy about it.

Well, there's no canceling now. You just confirmed that you were both going. Besides, if you cancel now, I'm sure she'd have your head.

Right? Should I wear a winter coat? She was very chilly. I'm a little scared.

You'll be fine. Just breathe.

Oh my God, why am I getting anxious about going out to meet my best friend?

Because she is being grumpy. She's not being very nice. You had reasons to cancel the last two weekends.

I can feel my heart rate speeding up and my chest tighten. My breath is shallow.

Maybe I should just cancel.

No! She'll be way more mad if you do.

But I shouldn't feel like this when I am just seeing my best friend.

Calm down. You will be fine when you get there.

Taking a deep breath, I open the closet door, pull out an outfit, get changed, and head down to the lobby to wait for my Road Trip.

I write a text message to McGruff. "Will you be at O'Brady's tonight? I'm going to meet Liz, but she seems mad, so I may need to make a swift exit."

O'Brady's is the pub across the street from Flannery's, my usual hang out on Saturday night. McGruff and his friends go there a lot, at least, they used to be there every Saturday. One of the ways he used to try to talk to me was by coming to Flannery's unexpectedly. He saw me there from across the street one night, and he just started showing up.

He responds as I'm climbing into the back seat of the red sedan. "Yes. But try to stay, Gem. I'm sure it will be fine. It's Liz."

It's Liz. I know it's Liz. I love Liz. But I hate when she's mad at me.

"Okay, see you in half an hour," I text back to McGruff.

"Gemma! Stay!"

Damn it. I liked it a lot more when I avoided talking to McGruff about my anxiety.

No, you didn't. You even thought about breaking up with him.

Right. But he wouldn't tell me to stay in an anxiety-inducing situation if I never told him about it.

No, because he didn't know. Besides, it's good for you to not run away from things. McGruff hates it when you run from him. It is much better now that you talk to him.

Fine. Yes, it is, but I'm still going to run away from Liz if I have to.

Running to McGruff instead of away. That is progress, even if you are running from your best friend.

I take a deep breath as the car pulls to a stop in front of Flannery's. Located on Boylston Street, it is an Irish pub, one of the many in Boston. The pub is on the small side, only twelve wooden tables are scattered over the wood floor, just up to the pool table and dart board. A long mahogany bar lines the wall, with televisions near the ceiling and a mirror that is nearly blocked by alcohol bottles ready to be poured.

Just breathe. It's just Liz.

She's here first, as usual, sitting at the bar with her arms crossed over her chest. Her golden, wavy hair flows down the back of the chair. I approach slowly and sit down next to her.

"Hey," I say.

"Hey," she responds, only glancing at me with her brown eyes.

Great. Is this how it's going to go all night? My eyes briefly flick towards the window in the direction of O'Brady's.

Just get it over with.

"Are you mad at me?" I ask.

She sighs heavily. "You've canceled on me the last two weekends, just like you did before."

"Liz, that was when my medication wasn't working. You were okay with it back then. This time I was so hungover from Foxwoods I couldn't even think of drinking on Saturday. And the next weekend, Nate's parents asked me to go to dinner with them in Salem. What was I supposed to say? Sorry I can't, I have to go drink with my best friend?"

"Oh, so I'm still your best friend?"

Ouch.

"Of course."

"It's not Brittany now?"

"No. If anyone, it would be Ed now."

She reluctantly smiles as Greg comes over with my drink. He's about six feet tall, with blue eyes and a blonde man bun. He scratches his chiseled jaw and asks, "Where have you two been?"

Ugh. Touchy subject, Greg.

I look at Liz. With her arms still crossed, she rolls her eyes.

"I've been busy," I respond.

Greg glances at Liz, then back at me, and then walks to the other end of the bar.

Damn it, Greg. I just had her smiling, and then you had to go and get her mad again. You can hide at the other end of the bar, but I can't.

You can run to O'Brady's.

So soon?

You've done it before.

"So do you *not* want to go out every Saturday now?" she asks.

Oh, shit. Why is she confronting me like this? What do I say?

The truth. Say the truth.

No, she'll definitely get madder.

You have to.

No. I'll just keep seeing her every Saturday until I die.

Gemma! Stand up for yourself.

"Well," I say softly. "I just don't think it's sustainable to meet every Saturday."

"Why? Because you're with Nate now? I come here every week, and I'm married."

"That's because Brett has poker night."

"Not every weekend."

"Yeah, because it's not sustainable."

Shit. I shouldn't have said that. She looks pissed.

"Nate sees his friends every Saturday," she replies.

"It's not every week anymore."

"Why? Because of you?"

Harsh.

"No. They just have their own lives. It's not that they don't want to. Them getting together just doesn't happen every week. But they still do, just not as often. And they're all okay with it. You were okay with us not meeting every Saturday night a few months ago."

142

"I was fine with it because you weren't feeling well, and your medication wasn't right. This is just you."

Ouch times five.

"Things change," I say.

"Things change?"

Oh, boy.

"I got married, and I still kept you in my life because you are my best friend, and I wanted to see you. You can't do that for me?"

"Liz, when you first started dating Brett, I barely saw you. Sure, it was a long time ago now, but really, it was only after you two got married that we started seeing each other every week. Before that, we got together when we were both free. When Brett started poker night, that's when we started our Saturday nights."

Good for you standing up for yourself!

"I can't believe you are choosing Nate over me."

"I'm not! I'm choosing both of you. I'm just saying that we may not be able to meet every single week. But I still want to meet."

"I can't do this right now," she says, drops a ten-dollar bill onto the bar, and walks out the door.

Look at that. She's the one running away today.

I watch her leave and then hang my head down to my chest.

"What was that about?" Greg asks.

"Apparently, I'm not a good friend anymore."

"Don't let it get you down. She'll get past it."

"Thanks. Can I get my check? And I guess hers, too."

"Leaving me already?"

"I am, sorry. I don't feel like sitting here alone."

"Oh, please. When you are here, you are never alone."

"Good point. But check, please?" I say and smile.

"Anything for you."

Sighing, I leave my money on the bar, twist out of my seat, and slowly walk across the street to O'Brady's. I find McGruff in the crowd, walk over, wrap my arms around him, nuzzle my face into his chest, and let his arms envelop me.

"Didn't go well?" he asks.

"No."

"I can see that this girl needs a drink," John says. He is tall and lanky, taller than McGruff, and has red hair. "I will go fetch one."

"Thanks, John," I say.

John smiles and walks to the bar.

"Where's Dan tonight?" I ask.

Dan is a coworker of McGruff's and a regular in his Saturday night crew.

"Had plans with his wife," George responds and tilts his head to the side. He has a pleasant round face with a bunch of freckles.

See, Dan can skip a week, and McGruff and the others aren't mad. Why is Liz?

"What happened?" Pete asks me.

Pete looks like a jock, but is more of a nerd. He has a blonde crew cut and broad shoulders that slump in my direction as he asks.

"Liz is mad at me," I say.

"We met her, right?" John asks as he reappears with my drink.

"Yeah, she was here the night…" I trail off.

"Oh! That night," Pete responds.

"The night we don't speak of," George says and laughs.

McGruff looks to the ceiling and sighs.

"Yes, that night," I respond and giggle.

That was the night McGruff and I got into a fight. For a little while, I was thinking of breaking up with him. But, as it turns out, it was good for us. I started to open up to him about my anxiety, and he did the same.

McGruff kisses the top of my head.

"Why's she mad?" John asks.

"Because I canceled on her two weeks in a row. And tonight, when I told her I didn't think I could see her every Saturday, she stormed out on me."

"Oh, boy," Pete says. "That's a tough one. I mean, I'd love to see these lads every week, and it was awesome when we could, but I understand when they can't make it."

"Yeah, give her time," George adds. "She will come around."

"I hope so. I feel like a terrible friend."

"Don't," John replies. "She shouldn't have walked out on you. This isn't all your fault. Takes two to tango."

"I guess you're right."

"I am *always* right," John says and laughs.

"Here we go," George responds.

"Smartest guy alive, over here." Pete motions towards John with his thumb and shakes his head.

"What? I am smarter than you three," John says.

"You left Gemma out," McGruff responds.

"Of course, I did. She's definitely smarter than all of us," John replies.

The guys do their best to make me laugh for a couple of hours before McGruff appeases me, and we go to his apartment.

Maybe you should have just said you'd see her every Saturday. Don't you want to?

Yes, but I also want to do other things, like these past two weekends. I don't want to feel like I have to go out with her. I don't want to feel like if I don't, she will get mad. I'm not good at being around people. I should just never leave my apartment.

You have to go to work, remember?

Ah, that. I can talk to HR about working from home forever.

You don't want to, though.

No, I don't. I am fine the way I am. I have worked my whole life to be normal like everyone else. I don't want to give in to my anxiety. I need to keep beating it down.

It's okay to ask for help.

Not like this. I'm not ready to wave the white flag and let my anxiety win.

It's not winning. You are just asking for help.

"What's that face for?" McGruff asks. "Thinking about Liz?"

"Surprisingly, no."

"What then?"

"I don't have a disability," I say.

McGruff half frowns and puts his palm on my cheek. "Gemma," he says, "you might. And that's okay."

"But…"

"I know you like to think of yourself as a warrior princess."

I roll my eyes.

"And you are," he continues, "but honey, you struggle with anxiety every day. And by struggle, I mean full-out wrestle with it. Most people don't do that. And yes, you are a warrior princess because of that. But you also may have a disability. Honestly, why not let someone help you? If the company will let you work from home because of your anxiety, if and only if, you call it a disability, then what is stopping you?"

"I am not weak."

"No one said you are. By God, you are one of the strongest people I know. If I had your anxiety, I would be curled up in my bed every day. But you, you fight, you conquer, you destroy what's in your path."

"I wouldn't go that far."

"I would."

"But I'm not…"

"There is nothing wrong with having a disability or anxiety, Gemma. Nothing at all. The Federal Government made this law to help people. They want to help you. So don't be so stubborn that you don't take the help."

"That was a bit harsh," I say and smile.

"Tough love, baby."

He curls his fingers around my hair.

"Okay. I guess I can see what you are saying," I say.

"Do you want to work in the office every day?"

"No."

"Then I guess we both know what you have to do."

"I guess so."

"Why don't you sound convinced?"

"Because I'm not. Things are so up in the air right now. Bob retiring. Me applying for a new job. I may wait. I am too anxious about everything else."

"That sounds reasonable, but just think about it. Okay?"

"Okay."

You already have your mind made up, don't you?

Shush. I can still think about my premade decision.

Oh, Gemma. Just keep it in the back of your mind, will you? In case things at work get too crazy again?

Yep. I will plop that thought right in the back of my mind.

You really are stubborn, aren't you? McGruff was right.

Just because I don't want to ask for help with something that secretly pummels me every day...Okay, yeah, I see it now.

Baby steps. Seeing Stacey and letting McGruff into your anxious thoughts were good progress. You can keep the ADA accommodation on the back burner for now. For now. Until you are ready to let go of the strangle hold you have on misperceptions about how to handle your anxiety.

Misperceptions? I am a warrior princess!

Yes, you are. But you don't always have to be.

CHAPTER ELEVEN

"We have to go all the way up. We're in the balcony," McGruff says.

"Yeah, Gemma, crappy seats," Nick taunts.

"Hey! It's the best I could get on short notice."

"I'm just kidding. All of the seats are great. You can see everything from everywhere."

"Unlike Fenway," McGruff adds. "When you can literally be sitting behind a pole."

Nick laughs. "So bad! I love Fenway Park, though."

I glance at Brittany, who returns my same look.

We have just arrived at TD Garden, the home to both the Boston Bruins and the Celtics. It also just so happens to be in the same place as North Station, where McGruff's family and I took the train to Salem. The trains leave from the ground level, obviously, but up a few escalators, and voila, we are in the round arena of the Garden. A large hallway circles the rink, or court as the case may be, and double doors open from the hallway into the stadium seating all around the rink.

"Should we get food before we sit?" Brittany asks.

"I like that idea," Nick replies.

"Me too," McGruff says.

As we get off the last escalator to the balcony level, the two guys walk ahead together, leaving Brittany and I a few paces behind.

"Is this weird?" Brittany asks.

"Oh, good. I thought it was just me."

"No. It's like we're not even here. Why *are* we even here?"

"They made us come along. And, actually, I bought the tickets. I should have just bought two."

For the two of them.

"Yeah, it's your fault," Brittany says and smiles.

I stop walking as we enter a huge corridor with concession stands circling the inside wall around the arena. We are a little early for the game, so there aren't hordes of people yet, just groups here and there in line for food and drinks and walking around trying to find the correct entrance into the auditorium to get to their seats. The corridor is oval, but large enough so that it still looks like a straight line until the built-in food stands disappear around the corner. Beers and wines, cheeseburgers, cheese steaks, chicken fingers, pizzas, and much more are being sold and bought all around us.

"What are you going to get?" Brittany asks me.

"Geez. I don't know. Maybe a burger."

"I was thinking that, too."

I scan the crowd for McGruff and Nick who are not in sight.

"Well, I guess the guys are going to take care of themselves."

"Who needs them?" Brittany jokes.

"Do you remember what seats we have?"

"Yep!"

"Then no one needs them! Not us!"

We pick the burger booth with the shortest line and are handed our burgers in paper cartons.

"Damn, these are the most expensive burgers I've ever bought," I say.

"Yeah, they won't taste like it, though," Brittany responds.

I look around at the standing height tables littered around the corridor. "Should we eat here or go in?" I ask.

"I would say we should go in and sit with the guys, but they probably haven't even noticed that we aren't there."

I sigh. "But we should, right?"

"Ugh! Yeah, we should go in and sit with them."

The guys are already seated next to each other and in conversation as we shimmy down the row with our burgers.

"Gem, you're over here," McGruff says and motions to the seat next to him on his left.

"Brittany, this is you," Nick says about the seat on his right.

I glance over my shoulder at Brittany as I crawl over both guys to sit on the other side of them while Brittany sits on the opposite end. Leaning back in my seat and looking behind the guys, I raise my eyebrows at Brittany.

"How did we let this happen?" Brittany mouths to me.

"I'm a moron," I mouth back.

Silently, I eat my food as McGruff and Nick talk about hockey and players that I've never heard of. The crowd quickly fills in all around us, and we are standing for the National Anthem.

A whistle sounds, and then a whole lot of commotion begins on the ice. The blue team skates into the black and gold team, which I am pretty sure are the Bruins. And then there is chaos and fighting. And more chaos.

I am sure there are rules, but I have no idea what they are. It just looks like a bunch of dudes skating into each other and then being allowed to fist fight on the ice.

That part is pretty cool actually. In what other sport can you just punch someone?

Boxing?

Shut up.

"Gem!" I hear Brittany shout past the guys. "I am going…"

"Yes!" I yell before she can even finish her sentence.

She smirks.

"Going out," I say to McGruff and squish by him as he barely even registers my presence.

"Oh, my God," Brittany says as we enter the quiet of the corridor. "I didn't realize it was so loud in there until we got out here."

I nod.

"Usually I like hockey, but Nick is barely speaking to me. He is so engrossed in the game. And with Nate," she adds.

I nod, again.

"Are you having fun?" she asks.

"I'm not having fun."

"I guess that'll do."

"What did you need to come out here for?" I ask.

"Oh, I had nothing. I just wanted to leave."

"Okay, great." I look around. "Well, we can still watch the game on one of these TVs." I point up the wall where there are televisions mounted up and down the hallways.

"Drink first?"

"Yes."

After paying for our expensive beers, we settle at a standing table near one of the televisions. The crowd inside roars, and I look up.

"We scored," Brittany says.

"I could have figured that out," I say and laugh.

"Just helping a girl out."

"So…what's up with you and Nick?"

"Ugh. I don't know! I was really excited about the game tonight, since it would be like a double date and the first time we've been out together since that time the three of us went to that bar. But tonight is more like a double date with Nick and Nate being one couple and you and I the other. Not what I was imagining at all."

"I'm sorry. Nate is pretty charming. Honestly, Nick could do a lot worse. Like *me* for example. That would have been way worse for him. I'm sorry you get stuck with me."

She smiles. "You are nothing like you think you are, Gemma Green."

I roll my eyes.

"He likes you, though," I say. "I can see it. Don't worry. You two will get together. I know it."

"Well, I'm glad one of us is sure."

"I am. You are cute together."

"Not as cute as Nick and Nate."

"Oh, my God! That is nothing. Trust me. You and I give them a run for their money. We are way cuter."

She laughs. "Yeah, we are."

Well, Brittany is anyway.

Shush. I was feeling good, and now that feeling is ruined.

Like when Jaqueline mentioned you could work from home forever and then called you disabled.

Again! Why do I do this to myself? I was feeling fine, and now I feel like poop.

I sigh and take a swig of my drink

Brittany tilts her head and raises an eyebrow. "You going to tell me what that sigh and that furrowed brow is about? You thinking about the job interview already? It hasn't even been set up yet, has it?"

No, but now I am.

Are you going to tell her?

Yes. She is my coworker, but she is also my friend.

Friend first. Coworker second.

Yes.

"Well, my meeting with the new VP…"

"Yes?" she prompts.

"I didn't tell you that she said there was a way for me to work from home full-time, maybe."

"That's great!" she says, but her face drops as she looks at me. "Why don't you seem like that's great?"

"Because it is covered under the Americans with Disabilities Act. I'd basically be saying that I have a disability that interferes with my life and my job, and I need to stay home to work to accommodate for that."

She looks silently at me and tilts her head to the other side. "Okay. You don't want to do that?"

"No, I don't."

"Why?"

"Because I am just like everyone else. I don't need special treatment."

I am fine the way I am!

"Gemma, yes you are like everyone else. No one is saying you aren't. But do me a favor and listen carefully as I repeat back what you said to me, okay?"

"Okay."

"You have *something* that interferes with your life and your job and you *would like* to stay home to *assist* you so you can work comfortably."

Well, when she says it like that.

"So?" she follows up.

"Those weren't my exact words."

"No, they weren't. But I said what you said."

"Yes."

"And what is incorrect with that statement about you?"

Shit. Nothing. Literally nothing. I have something that interferes with my life and my job, and I would like to stay home to assist me so I can work comfortably.

"Nothing."

"Right. Why does it matter that it's being called a disability?"

Why do I have such smart friends? I should just live in a hole like I've always wanted.

I mumble, barely audible, "It doesn't matter."

Brittany leans forward. "What was that?"

"It doesn't matter," I say a little louder.

"I still can't hear you."

"It doesn't matter!" I shout.

"Yes! It does not matter!" she shouts back.

"Now yell out that you have a disability."

"What? No."

"Why not?"

"Because I don't have one."

"Didn't we just talk about this?"

"I don't want to offend people."

"Okay, okay. Yell out that you have an anxiety disorder."

"No, I don't want people to know."

"Why not? Plus, all these people are strangers. You will never see them again."

She's got a point. Why not own this disability/disorder of yours? And maybe take it a step further and ask HR about that accommodation.

One thing at a time.

"So?" Brittany asks.

"Okay. I have an anxiety disorder."

"That was pathetic. I barely heard you."

"I have an anxiety disorder!"

"Better. But I want you to yell it."

Yell it?

Why not girl? Own this shit.

I raise my arms and shout, "I have an anxiety disorder!"

Everyone around us stops and stares at me.

"A little too loud," Brittany whispers.

I collapse my arms around my chest and start laughing. Hysterically laughing. Brittany joins in with me.

"What is so funny out here?" Nick asks as he and McGruff walk over to our table.

"You had to be here," Brittany says.

"Game over?" I ask.

McGruff smiles down at me. "No, it's the end of the first period."

"How many periods?" I ask.

"Three," he responds.

Two more of these!

Thank goodness it was an afternoon game. McGruff can still help me practice for my interview which is tomorrow, but all I can think

154

about is Liz. It's been a day since I've talked to her. I usually talk to her every single day, and I'm too much of a coward to text her because I know she is still mad at me. And next weekend...

"What are you thinking about?" McGruff asks me. He puts his hand on my knee and leans against the couch.

"Friendsgiving."

"It's next weekend, right?"

"Yep."

"Why so glum?"

"Liz is going to kill me. I don't even want to text her to tell her that I can't go out on Saturday. Again."

"Invite her to come?"

"She's never met Walter."

"I think they'd like each other."

"Plus, she'd either refuse or start a fight with me in the middle of dinner."

"Maybe she'll cancel for Saturday first."

"Maybe. But I have a feeling she is going to wait and see if I cancel. And if I don't, she won't show up just to spite me."

"You really think Liz would do that?"

"No. I just feel bad. I hate that she doesn't want to talk to me."

"You're going to have to text her. She will be even madder if you don't text, and she shows up and you're not there."

"I know."

"Hey," he says and places his hand on my cheek. "It'll be okay. I promise. Liz is your best friend."

"It had better be okay. The last time we got into a fight, she didn't talk to me for weeks."

You didn't talk to her either, remember?

"She'll be fine once she cools down."

I sigh. "Okay, so will you help me practice now?"

"But of course," he replies and scans the room.

"What are you looking for?"

"A good place to practice. I could sit on one side of the breakfast bar and you on the other?"

"That works," I mumble.

"Hey! Everything is going to be fine. Don't make me tickle you," he shouts and makes a move in my direction.

I flinch and yell, "No! You know how much I hate being tickled!"

"I know! But I love forcing you to smile and laugh."

"So cruel."

"Cruel?"

"Yeah. Tickling is cruel. I can't explain it. But it is. Even though it makes me laugh."

"Whatever you say, sugar."

"Sugar?" I ask and tilt my head to the left.

"Was that weird?"

"No, I liked it."

"Okay, sugar."

I smile as I sit across from him. He pulls his seat close to the breakfast bar and casually folds his hands on the counter in front of him.

"Okay, Ms. Green," he says. "Tell me why you want this job."

Oh, shit. Why do I want this job? I can't say because I hate my current one. I also can't say because I hate running meetings and don't want to be a project manager.

"Ms. Green?"

"I...shit, Nate. I'm never going to get this job. I don't even know why I want it."

"Gemma," he says and reaches across the counter and grabs my hand. "Yes, you do. Just breathe. Why do you want this job?"

"I am very interested in and enjoy coding, specifically in SQL and would like to learn more."

"Good! Why should we hire you?"

"I've been with the company for five years. I know our data, our warehouse, our systems, and our company very well."

"Do you have any experience with SQL?"

"Yes, as a BA, I pull my own data with SQL queries."

"Where do you see yourself in five years?"

Definitely not as a project manager.

"As a warehouse developer at this company."

McGruff smiles. "Well, I'd hire you."

"You have to say that. You're my boyfriend."

"Honestly, I don't see how they wouldn't hire you. You know everything about the company, systems, and data. You're a business analyst, so you've mapped or created requirements for all of it. Plus, you're very smart and already know how to code. Everyone loves you, and you are incredibly adorable."

"Shut up."

"All of that is true."

"What if someone with more warehouse experience applies?"

"That is possible. But I still like your chances. You know so much; it really impresses me. The other candidates are going to have to be superstars if they are going to beat you."

"Stop..."

"Never."

"You're a huge dork."

"I know. That's why you like me."

"Yep. Just that one reason."

"Just the one, huh?"

"Mmhmm."

Before I can react, he sprints to my side of the breakfast bar, wraps his arms around me, and tickles me.

"No!" I scream. "I take it back. There are no reasons I like you!"

"Oh!" He stops abruptly, his arms still around me. "None?"

"Nope," I say.

I can feel his hands moving up my back and his fingers twirling in my hair as he pulls me closer to him. I feel his hot breath on my skin right before his lips touch mine.

CHAPTER TWELVE

Oh, for the love of God, why didn't I cancel this God forsaken meeting? My interview is this afternoon. I don't need the extra stress caused by a meeting I can't run, even though I'm supposed to, and by Jack who makes it worse by being Jack.

You didn't cancel because you have this horrible thing called work ethic. You really need to push that aside in times like these. You need to put yourself before your job sometimes. Work on that.

"Hey, Gemma," Joe says as he enters.

Nick walks in right behind him, followed by Ed, who closes the door behind himself.

"What about Jack?" I ask.

"Oh," Ed says as he sits. "I took the liberty of telling Jack that he's not needed today."

"And he just believed you?" I ask.

"Of course, he did. He's Jack," Ed replies.

"You're kind of the best," I say.

"What about me?" Nick asks.

"Did you tell Jack he didn't have to come?" Ed inquires.

Nick frowns and says quietly, "No."

"There you have it," Ed responds. "But I would like it noted to the court that she only said '*Kind of* the best.'"

I smirk. "You know you're the best of the best," I say.

"Again! What about me?" Nick asks.

"Geez," Ed says. "Aren't you jealous today?"

"Only because Gemma is joining you in the data warehouse group and won't be on projects with me anymore." Nick crosses his arms and leans back in his chair

"Not yet. I haven't even interviewed."

"Oh!" Ed says. "When is it?"

"This afternoon."

Completely confused, Joe asks, "What's the interview for?"

"For Larry's job," I respond.

"Who are you interviewing with?" Ed asks.

"Andy and Roger."

"Ew," Ed responds.

"What? Is that bad?" I ask.

"No, it's expected. Roger would be your manager, too, then huh?"

"If all goes well."

"We will be teammates!" Ed shouts.

"Again, don't be so excited!" Nick shouts back.

"Oh, come on. Be happy for Gemma," Ed says.

"I am. Really, I am."

"Do you think they will be hard on me?" I ask.

"Hard to say. They know you, which helps. And I am sure you've worked with them before, so they know your work ethic."

"So, you're saying she's a shoo-in," Joe says.

"I don't want to get everyone's hopes up, I mean besides Nick's, but I think she is, yes. They'd be crazy not to hire her."

Am I turning red? I think I'm turning red.

"Any advice?" I ask.

"Just be yourself," Nick says. "That's all you need to do, and you will be fine."

That's horrible advice. Has he even met me?

"Roger is more technical," Ed replies. "He may ask you how to code in SQL just to see where your skill level is at. Andy will probably ask how your current job would transfer over to being a data warehouse developer, why you want to switch, and so on."

"I think I can handle that," I respond.

"Of course, you can!" Nick says. "They are idiots if they don't hire you."

"Honestly, Gemma," Ed adds, "The interview is probably just a formality. They already know you. They already know you can do the job. Just don't completely blow the interview, and you are in."

"Okay. Well, odds are you just jinxed me, and I will."

"Damn it, Ed," Joe responds. "Why did you say that?"

Yeah, Ed! You know that I will act like a fool now just because you told me not to.

Actually, you would have done it anyway.

Point taken.

"No, no, no!" Ed reacts. "Gemma will do fine!"

Obviously, doesn't know me well enough.

"Of course, she will," Nick says.

"Yes, she will," Joe adds on.

They all look at me and smile.

"Besides," Ed says, "You've got my recommendation."

"Your recommendation is worth shit!" Nick says.

"Oh, come on," Ed replies. "I will quit if Gemma doesn't get the job!"

"Did you tell them that?" Joe asks.

"Yes."

"Damn it, Ed," Nick says. "That guarantees she won't get the job now."

"Hey!" Ed replies. "They like me. They really, really like me."

"Just keep telling yourself that," Joe says.

"Stop," Ed says. "This is about Gemma."

Actually, I liked it better when they were talking about Ed. Can we go back to that? I don't want to think about the interview, or I will panic.

Just wait until the time arrives.

Shush! I will be fine.

Stop it. Are you panting? Stop this right now.

I can't. I'm so nervous. What if they ask me questions I don't know the answers to?

Then you say that you don't know but you are sure that you can figure it out.

What if I projectile vomit?

Then, you probably won't get the job. Just breathe. You will be fine. You just need to talk to two people whom you have spoken to many times before.

Not in this situation.

No, but you've had to present and lead meetings. Just act like you don't care.

Never in the history of the world has that ever worked. My body never pays any attention to what my mind is telling it. It will have a conniption fit if it wants to, all the while my brain will be telling it that everything is fine.

Everything *is* fine.

What did I just say? That won't work.

Oh my, God. I'm going to throw up.

No, you're not. Just breathe.

I drop my chin to my chest and breathe. I can feel my heartbeat pulsing throughout my head. I'm getting dizzy.

Stop this right now! You will not pass out. You will not vomit. You will march your tushy into that conference room and be the bad ass bitch you know you can be.

Taking another deep breath, I lift my head and lock my computer.

Just get up. Just stand up. One step at a time. Just get yourself to the conference room. Do it!

After another deep breath, I stand. My limbs get weak, and my head floats, but I still walk to the conference room, sit down, and wait.

I hate waiting. My body has time to wind itself into a knot, ready to unravel at lightning speed at any moment.

Relax. Relax your neck. Relax your shoulders. Relax.

"Hey, Gemma."

My eyes flip to the door to see Roger enter and close the door behind him.

Shit, it's happening.

"How are you doing?" he asks as he sits directly across from me.

"Good. How are you?"

"I am great," he says as he nonchalantly leans back in his seat, rests his hands on the arms of the chair, and crosses his legs. He lets out a little yawn and pats himself twice on the chest.

Oh, to be that carefree.

"All right," he says, looking at me with his hazel eyes, almost the same color as his dark blonde hair. "I really like internal interviews so much more than external, you know? I already know you. I don't have to ask stupid getting-to-know-you questions."

Oh, thank God.

"We can just get to the good stuff," he adds.

The good stuff? What the hell is the good stuff?

"Do you get to do any SQL coding as a BA?" he asks.

Question one. Just as Ed predicted, technical information.

"Yes. I know a lot of BAs don't, but I like to dig into what I am writing requirements for, so that I completely understand the processes I am documenting. I hate when there are still questions about how something works or how something should work when the programming is in progress."

"I like that answer, Gemma. Honestly, I have heard that about you. You are one of the best BAs anyone has worked with."

Well, I'll be damned.

"How confident are you in building databases? DDL, DML, DCL?"

Not at all confident. I don't even know what those stand for.

"Well, as a BA I don't have any opportunity to do that, but I am sure I can pick it up quickly."

"Okay. How would you troubleshoot database issues?"

Uh.

"Well, the way I would any issue. I would first try to understand it, find the root cause, and trace the issue from there until I can find a solution for it."

That was some nice BS, Gemma.

"Would you know how to build a View?"

No. I don't.

"As I said, I don't have much access to SQL as a BA, but I am sure I can figure it out."

Damn it. This isn't going well.

"Have you ever worked with cloud databases?"

Shit.

"No."

"Do you know the different types of joins used in SQL?"

Finally, something I know.

"Yes, inner, left, right, cross."

"What about primary keys? Unique keys? Do you know what they are?"

"Yes, a primary key ensures that each row in the database is distinct. The unique key is similar, but it allows null values."

"Do you feel like you could step into this role and immediately be able to perform at a high level?"

No! Why am I even interviewing for this job?

"I think there will be some time when I need to learn some things about SQL that I don't know, but I am confident I can learn it quickly."

Are you confident, though?

As he asks more and more questions, I feel my confidence level waning. There is no way I am getting this job.

Chin up, Gemma. Maybe Andy will like you.

I wait in silence for Andy to arrive and give me the third degree.

Don't think like that. You need to stay positive.

"Hi, Gemma," he greets me and sits. He looks kindly at me with his brown eyes and asks, "How is it going so far? Roger treat you okay?"

He treated me like any other interviewee who was looking for a data warehouse developer job, so I guess, yes?

"It is going well."

Liar!

"Good, good. I don't think I'm going to take the full thirty minutes here, since I already know you."

Praise the lord.

"So, tell me why you want this job."

My mind goes blank.

Gemma, you know this. Come on, you know this. Say something. Say anything.

Oh, my God. Why do I want this job? Because I hate my current one?

Gemma! Say something!

It's back. I can feel my anxiety boiling up my body, reaching my neck, and my head.

Breathe! You have to say something!

Choking back nausea, I say, "This is the path I'd like to take with my career. I've been a BA for years now, and I've found that I really enjoy SQL and coding, and I'd like to do it full time."

Not bad. Not bad, Gemma. Just continue to breathe and not vomit.

"Does anything from your current job translate to being a data warehouse developer?"

"I do some SQL querying, and I am familiar with our databases and servers."

"Good. What would you say to someone who thinks we should hire a candidate with a data warehouse development background over you who is coming to us as a BA?"

I would say that is an absolutely solid idea. I mean, I would hire someone who knows what they are doing over me. It's a no-brainer.

Gemma, do not say that. I beg of you.

"I would say that I know our systems, our data, our warehouse, our processes almost as well as anyone else at this company. It takes less time to learn a few lines of code than it does to learn all of that."

That was so good, Gemma. You sounded so confident and forceful.

His eyes are definitely smiling at me.

CHAPTER THIRTEEN

Sighing heavily, I slam the potato masher down onto the counter. Why did I agree to make something? I should have just bought mashed potatoes and put them in one of my own dishes. Now, I've ruined them, and everyone will laugh at me, and worst of all, we won't have mashed potatoes for Friendsgiving.

I spin around when there's a knock on my door. "Come in!" I yell and McGruff enters my apartment with a bowl of stuffing and a pumpkin pie.

"You made both of those?" I ask.

He places them both onto the counter and answers, "No, just the stuffing. I bought the pie. How's it going in here?"

"Terrible."

"Let me take a look," he says and gently moves me out of the way so he can inspect the potatoes. "Hmm. Still a little lumpy, huh? Okay." He takes the masher and presses the potatoes until they are creamy. "There we go. Not so terrible after all. You cooked the potatoes and heated with the butter. You did the hard stuff. Just needed a little brute force."

"Well, I'm glad you were here."

He smiles at me, and his eyes twinkle.

"Did you invite, Liz?" he asks.

"I did. She politely declined."

"It'll be okay," he says and runs his hand through my hair.

"I hope so. She didn't really seem mad."

This time.

That's probably because you invited her and didn't exclude her.

She still said no.

But nicely. She's coming around. Just you wait and see.

"You ready?" McGruff asks.

"Ready as I'll ever be."

"Don't forget the wine," he says and points to the bottle behind me on the counter.

As if I could ever forget my life blood.

Okay, yeah, now I can see why McGruff is worried about my drinking. I just called wine my life blood.

Only because you need it to get through social situations.

Do I though? I know and love these people. I use alcohol as a crutch without even thinking about it. Maybe my meds are actually working, and I don't even know it because I always default to drinking.

Just don't drink a lot.

When we get to Walter's door, I can already hear laughter coming from inside. McGruff knocks, and Josh opens the door.

"Gemma! So good to see you. And you must be Nate," he says and shakes McGruff's hand, "I'm Joshua."

"Nice to meet you, Joshua," McGruff replies.

See, McGruff has no problem calling him Joshua instead of Josh. Just be cool this time and say his name properly.

"Hi, Joshua. Good to see you again," I say.

Good. You didn't stumble over his name like you did last time he was here.

That was only because Walter calls him Josh, and he calls himself Joshua. I am accustomed to hearing his name as Josh, but wanted to say it properly to his face.

Well, it didn't go well.

"Hey!" Walter and Sally cheer when we walk in.

"Fashionably late," Sally says.

"My potatoes needed a little CPR," I respond.

Josh takes the bottle of wine from my hand and replaces it with a glass of poured wine.

I love this man.

I place the mashed potatoes onto the table as McGruff puts his stuffing and pie down, too.

"Nate, wine?" Josh asks.

"Yes, please."

"Turkey won't be done for a little while, so come sit," Walter says. "I have cheese and crackers over here on the coffee table, and Sally brought some spanakopita."

"Oh, Sally," McGruff says. "If only I could have found me a girl who could cook."

Everyone looks at me and smirks.

"There's still time," I say as I sit between Walter and Sally on the couch.

McGruff smiles and sits in a chair opposite me. "Don't even want to sit next to me now?"

"Not anymore," I say as I take an appetizer dish and put a couple squares of spanakopita onto it.

"How have you been, Nate?" Walter asks.

"Very good. My parents came to town a couple of weeks ago."

"Oh, I heard about that," Walter says.

"Did you now?" McGruff replies and looks at me.

"Only good stuff," I respond.

"Yes, she told me that you kept your birthday from her, and your parents had to tell her."

"Mostly good stuff," I say.

"And that you went to Salem," Walter continues.

"How is Salem?" Josh asks.

"It is a mecca for Halloween lovers around the world," McGruff answers.

"So...?" Josh asks for more.

"It was crowded and crazy," I say. "But Nate's dad took charge," I add and dramatically drink a sip of wine.

What was that comment for? McGruff is eyeing you right now. Don't make eye contact.

168

"I've always wanted to take my daughter, Julia, there," Josh replies.

"Don't let me dissuade you. It's very cool," I say.

"Yes, please bring your daughter next time," Sally adds.

"I will. I want this one to come to New York City more often, though," Josh says and points at Walter.

No, I knew this was going to happen. You can't take him to New York. I won't let you.

He's Walter's son. Walter may actually want to move there to be closer to his family.

Stop. I couldn't take it.

"You had fun in Salem, then?" Sally asks, looking at me and then at McGruff.

"I did," McGruff says and looks pointedly at me.

"What? I did, too. We all went into a haunted house and came out hysterically laughing," I say and take another sip of wine.

What are you doing? You are making Friendsgiving weird and there is no reason for it to be weird.

"Yeah, we did," McGruff responds, "because Gemma was still scared when we came out and jumped when my mom tapped her shoulder."

Everyone laughs.

"What? It could have been a goblin. I didn't know."

McGruff smiles and says, "We all had fun."

"Sounds like it," Sally replies. "What did you think of Nate's parents?" Sally asks me.

Oh, no. Loaded question.

"Jen is so nice and sweet. I really like her."

They all keep staring at me.

They are waiting for you to say something about his dad.

What do I say about Sir Thomas?

Don't know. But the longer you wait, the weirder this is going to get.

"His dad was…as expected."

As expected? What does that even mean?

McGruff tilts his head and scrunches his face. Everyone else slowly nods.

Oh, goodness, Gemma. You should have just said he was nice, too. Now look at them staring awkwardly.

We are all sitting in silence.

What the crap, Gemma?

"How's the café, Sally?" Josh finally asks.

"Good! I'm so much happier now that I close in the early afternoon. I can get so much more done in my days."

"I bet."

"Don't see these three quite as much anymore. That's the only downside," Sally says, pointing to me, McGruff, and Walter.

"What do you do for work, Nate?" Josh asks.

"I'm a computer programmer. I work in the same building as our little Gemma here."

Again, they all look at me and smile.

I'm suddenly wishing McGruff hadn't come with me. The last get together here at Walter's did not start with me being the entertainment for the group. They barely even knew I was here last time. I just drank the wine.

They just love you, Gemma. Deal with it.

I take another sip of wine.

"Have you heard anything about the job, Gemma?" Sally asks.

"Not yet. I am hoping soon."

"New job?" Josh inquires.

"At the same company," I reply. "I applied to be a data warehouse developer."

"That's great! Good luck!"

"Thank you."

"How do you think the interview went?" Walter asks.

Honestly, pretty crappy.

Don't say that. You don't believe it. You had Andy on your side.

"It wasn't the greatest. But I think one of the guys liked me."

"It will all work out, honey, I know it," Sally says.

I wish I was that optimistic about it.

"I hear you work from home a couple days, Gemma?" Josh asks.

"Yes, Monday and Friday."

"How do you like that? It's a change, I'm sure."

"It is, but I get to spend Monday mornings with Walter. It doesn't get much better than that."

"Nonsense," Walter says.

"Do you miss being in the office every day?" Josh inquires.

Oh heck no.

"Only on the rare occasion when something cool happens."

"What cool things happen at the office?" Sally asks.

I see them all smirk.

"Like when the sprinklers went off in the conference room, and we all had to be evacuated because the HVAC system caught on fire. I'd be bummed if I missed that."

Shush. That's when Nick almost kissed you.

Well, I'm obviously not going to say that.

"Wasn't it only your conference room where the sprinklers went off?" McGruff asks.

"No, there were others," I say.

They all smirk again.

"Honestly, Gemma would rather spend every day at home instead of the office," McGruff says to Josh.

I shrug.

"What did Gemma get you for your birthday, Nate?" Sally asks, changing the subject.

"She got me tickets to a Bruins game."

"That's nice! Just the two of you?" Sally follows up.

"Uh, no. She brought two of her coworkers."

"Gemma! Not even his own friends?" Sally replies.

"No, but in my defense, he and Nick did say they wanted to go to a Bruins game. I just stupidly made it happen."

"It was not stupid! I had a lot of fun," McGruff says.

"I know. I am glad Nick went because you had way more fun with him than you would have with me."

"Gemma!" everyone says at the same time.

Literally everyone, even Josh.

"What? It's the truth, and I am okay with it."

Their shocked looks all turn to smiles.

"I had a very good time with everyone," McGruff politely adds.

A timer dings from the kitchen, and Walter hesitantly gets up from his seat and walks over to the oven.

"Josh, will you help me carve the turkey?"

"Of course, dad."

After a few minutes of hushed bickering and cussing, we are called over to the table.

"Turkey looks great," I say.

Before I sit, Josh refills my glass and then McGruff's. McGruff can't blame me for drinking more. It would be rude to refuse, especially since it's already in my glass.

Gemma, you just need to be aware of your drinking while on medication. McGruff is not mad.

I peek at McGruff out of the corner of my eye. He is taking a sip of his own wine.

See, he's good.

"Okay," Walter says. "I want to do a little toast before we start. I want to say how thankful I am to have each of you in my life. You all bring me so much joy. I can never express how much you all mean to me. I want you to remember that no matter where life may take any one of us. Cheers."

"Cheers," we all respond and raise our glasses.

No, I don't like that toast. That toast has a hidden meaning. He's going to move to New York City to be with his family, isn't he? Well, we're his family too, McGruff, Sally and I.

I feel McGruff place his hand on my knee and squeeze. He knows too. It's the beginning of the end.

Remove that from your mind, Gemma. Just be happy in the moment. Do not ruin today with your thoughts.

Never has there been any day when I did not ruin the day with my thoughts.

Well, give this one a shot, will you?

Sure, I will try to not think of my beloved Walter moving away from me.

What did I just say!

"This is all delicious, Walter," McGruff says.

"Thank you," Walter replies, "but I can't take all the credit. You all brought scrumptious food, as well."

"More wine, Gemma?" Josh asks.

Oh shit, my glass is empty again.

"No, thank you. I think I've had enough."

Good for you!

"I will get you some water, then," Josh responds.

"Perfect, thank you."

I can feel McGruff looking at me, but I don't look back.

Is he surprised, shocked, concerned?

"How was the Bruins game?" Sally asks McGruff. "What do you think of Brittany and Nick?"

"It was good. We lost unfortunately, but I had a good time. And I really like them. They are good people."

"Yes, they are. They have a bit of a thing happening," Sally says and looks at me.

"A thing?" Josh asks.

"They are becoming more than friends," Sally responds.

"Ah," Josh replies.

"Gemma, how do you feel about that?" Sally asks me.

Now why would she purposefully do that to me?

"I'm getting used to it," I respond.

"I think she feels a little left out," Sally explains to every one else. "But I told her that you and Nate acted the same when you first met."

"We weren't nearly as nauseating, were we?" I ask.

"Well, no," McGruff says, "because I could barely get you to talk to me, never mind sit at the same table with me."

Everyone laughs, and I reluctantly smile.

"Oh!" McGruff continues. "I did learn something recently. When we first met, Gemma used to call me McGruff!"

Silence. Looks are exchanged around the table.

"You all knew?" McGruff shouts.

They all snicker.

"Yeah, you used to come into my café," Sally offers. "And would we chat about it."

"Yeah," Walter adds. "We used to talk about you."

Josh shrugs. "My dad told me."

"Come on!" McGruff shouts.

Everyone laughs. This time not at me.

Thank goodness for that.

But McGruff keeps side eyeing me all night.

"What?" I say as the door closes to Walter's apartment, and we make the small journey back down the hall to my apartment.

"What? What?"

"You know what. You've been looking at me funny all night."

"It seemed like you had fun. And without too much alcohol. I was just surprised that you chose to stop drinking," he says as we close the door to my own apartment.

Surprised! That was the look.

"Well, you've been upset with me every time I drink, so I decided I wouldn't drink as much tonight."

"Gemma," he says softly and takes my hand. "I'm not upset. I'm just worried about you. You technically aren't supposed to be drinking on your medication, and the last few times I've seen you drink, you've gotten very drunk, and it scares me."

"When?"

"When you called me at Foxwoods, when you didn't respond to me at Foxwoods the next night, at Bob's retirement party, the night Liz got mad at you…:"

"Okay, Okay. I get it. I drink too much."

"No, you don't. You just can't drink as much now as you used to. It hits you differently. I just want you to be safe. That's all. I worry about you. So much."

I sigh and look up into his gorgeous blue, emotional eyes.

"I get it."

"And you made a comment about my father tonight, too."

I knew he was going to say something about that.

"I'm sorry. I don't even know what I meant by it. I shouldn't have said it."

"But you were right. He did take charge. He always does."

I don't understand. Is he mad at me or not?

He takes my hand and leads me to the couch, and I sit next to him.

"Did you not like him?" he asks, his eyes big and vulnerable. "I know I've said a lot about him in the past. But I'd like it if you got along with my family."

"No! It's not like that at all."

"So, he didn't make you anxious?"

"Oh, yeah he definitely did. But I liked him. I did."

"Really? I know I talk a lot of crap about him, but he's my dad."

"I know. And I can tell that he loves you, too. It's not how most people show love, but it is there, and I saw it. He even told me that you are a good man, and he is only hard on you because he wants you to be the best man you can be."

"Deep down I know that," he says, sighs, and hangs his head.

"What is it?" I ask.

"I just don't want to be like him. I mean, not like that. I want people to know how I feel about them. And sometimes I don't know if my feelings come out right. Like a few months ago when we got into the fight at O'Brady's."

"Oh, Nate. You are nothing like your father in that way. You are so gentle and show you care so much. You don't have to worry about that."

"Good. Good. Because…good."

Because good?

Gemma, do not stress about his wording.

Nope. I think I will.

CHAPTER FOURTEEN

As the apartment door slowly creaks open, I turn to see Walter mosey in with two coffees in hand. He closes the door with his hip before I can stand up from my desk and walk over to help.

"Hey kid," he says and hands me a cup.

"Morning, Walter. Josh still asleep?"

"Yes, stayed up late working, poor kid."

"When is your train again?"

"Not until tomorrow night. I think he wants a couple days off without traveling. Plus, I think he might like it here," he says, smiles, and then winks.

He shuffles over to the couch, and I unplug my laptop and move it from my desk to the coffee table. Sitting down next to Walter, I lean back and sigh.

"What's on your mind?" Walter asks.

"A few things."

"I see. You seem pretty stressed for so early in the morning. Put down your coffee," he says. He points to my cup as he places his own on the table. "We can talk after."

I obey and follow his lead as he goes through all of the tai chi moves that the instructor has taught us when we go to the sessions at Frog Pond.

My breathing slows as I stretch my arms in the air and make the subtle motions of each pose. We sit in silence for a few moments when we are finished with our routine.

"Feeling better?" Walter asks.

"I am."

"Good. Now what's first on the list to discuss?"

I sigh. "Liz."

"Still haven't talked to her about the fight?"

"No. But she hasn't talked to me either."

"That's no excuse. Just because she hasn't said anything doesn't mean you can't."

"I know. But I don't know what else to say. I haven't changed my mind about anything that I said to her."

"Maybe she has."

"I kind of doubt it."

"Still. She's your best friend. You will smooth it over. I'm sure of it."

I wish I was that sure.

"She was really mad, Walter."

"Like I said, kid, you will get past it."

"I really hope so."

"Next item on the list?"

"The job I interviewed for."

That reminds me to reach over to my laptop, move the cursor, and check to see if I have any new emails. I don't.

"When do you expect to hear back?"

"Sometime this week, I hope."

If it's any longer, I will probably worry myself until I disintegrate.

"How are you feeling about it?"

"Sometimes really good. Other times really bad. It could go either way."

"Gemma, you are one of the smartest people I have ever met, and I've met a few. I have no doubt that you will get the job."

"Thanks, but I'm not so sure."

"Okay, and if you don't, then you will find another job, either at the same company or at another one that will make you happy. You are too young to be so unhappy, especially with your job. There are so many jobs out there in the world. You can find one that you enjoy more than the one you have right now."

He's right. If you don't get this job, you can find another one at another company, one that will let you work remotely full time. If you don't get this job, it's not the end of the world. You are not stuck at KPM, and you are not stuck as a business analyst or, God forbid, a project manager.

I am not defined by my job, even though sometimes I feel like I am. No matter how much I feel like a moron at my job, that is not me. I am not my job, and my job is not me.

You are so much more than your job. Just because you get anxious and act oddly at work doesn't mean that you are odd.

I am not my anxiety, either.

But, man, I hope I get the job. I really like the people I work with. I would miss them if I left the company.

"Gemma? Are you okay?"

Damn. I've gone comatose again.

"Yeah. Just letting what you said sink in. You're right. I shouldn't be afraid to get a new job or apply at a new company."

"You don't even need to stay in Boston."

And there it is, the third item on my list.

"So, I'm guessing that you are moving to New York City to be close to Josh?"

He remains silent for a moment, and then says, "I don't want to leave you, Gemma. You or Sally or Nate. But I think I have to. I'm getting old, too old, to be living so far from family."

"I'm your family."

"I know. But I don't want to burden you. What if something happened to me?"

"You're not a burden. I would help you no matter what."

"I know," he says softly and puts his hand on mine. "But I don't want you to have to. I want you to live your life the way you want to. I want you to be happy."

"I'm happy with you here."

"I know, kid. And I'm happy with you here, too. You will just have to visit any chance you get."

It won't be the same.

"I will. I promise."

My laptop chimes, and I lift it from the table.

"Meeting?" Walter asks.

"Yep."

I hit the join meeting button and wait in cyberspace until Carl remembers that I am supposed to be in this meeting and logs in from the conference room computer.

Ding. "Hi, Gemma," Carl says.

"Hi Carl," I reply and mute myself for what I hope will be the remainder of the meeting.

I honestly can't wait until I never have to go to these meetings again.

You will go to some.

Yes, but I won't have to take meeting notes, and I won't be invited to meetings that I am clearly not needed in because Carl thinks he needs a business analyst and that I should act more like a project manager.

"That's not it!" I hear Jack yell, and despite the fact that he is probably sitting far from the phone, I can still hear him loud and clear.

That's another thing I won't miss. Jack. Unless I'm on a project with him, I will probably never interact with him again. The fact that I'm new makes me think that I won't be on projects any time soon, and if I am, I will still be working from home part time so it won't be too bad.

Oh, my God! Say that again!

No meetings with Jack.

Yes!

Walter's eyes pop open and he looks at me as Jack yells again.

I shrug.

Yes, I cannot wait until I no longer have to deal with him.

A message pops up from Nick. "Any word?"

Oh, right, I haven't gotten the job yet. Let's roll this thought process back a few pegs. I don't even know if I will be working from home part time. I know that Jaqueline said it was most likely to continue, but it's not a definite. My new manager has to approve it.

At least, I have some things to talk to Stacey about after work tonight.

Walter stands, waves, and walks towards the door as Jack yells again. I wave back and mouth, "Sorry."

Typing back to Nick, I write, "Nope."

"Damn, they are really drawing this out," he types back.

Yes, they are. There is no word on the job all day. Taking my disappointment in stride, I head out to get a Road Trip after work.

Placing my purse onto the chair next to me, I turn to look at Stacey, who is scratching her chin and looking quizzically at me.

"I see you didn't bring Nate today," she says.

No, where would he sit? That chair is for my purse and only my purse.

"No, there was some other stuff going on, and we talked about the drinking and about his dad. Looking back, I'm not sure why I was so upset about his dad. Sure, he made me uncomfortable, but he was nice in his own way. I just need to get used to it."

"Okay. Sounds like you made some progress. Since you mentioned him, let's talk about Nate's dad."

Ugh. Why did you mention him?

"Okay…"

Does she want me to talk? Because I've said all I wanted to say about him.

"The last time you were here, you weren't sure what a future relationship with Nate would be like when his dad made you uncomfortable."

Yes. I believe I already addressed that.

"Yeah. I was dwelling on the things that made me anxious and not the whole picture. I know his father cares about him. Nate and I talked. He doesn't want to turn out like his father, and I don't think that there's a chance he will."

"So, you don't feel uncomfortable around Nate's father?"

"Oh, I do. I definitely do. I just don't think it will get in the way of a relationship with Nate. Nate isn't very keen on him either. And I did see a side of his father that made me understand where he was coming from."

"You did? What happened? Was this after you went to Salem?"

"No. It was in Salem. I didn't bring it up last time."

"Why not?"

I was too wrapped up by being in his military now.

"I was too wrapped up in how anxious I was around him. He told me in his own way, that he loves Nate and just wants to bring out the best in him."

"I see. And you didn't take that into consideration before?"

Guess not. I'm only human.

Human-ish.

"No. I remembered that I feel less awkward around people when I get to know them more, and maybe that will happen with Nate's dad."

Fingers crossed. I did see a glimmer of hope in Salem.

Come on, you like him.

"Okay. And last time you were worried about how Nate reacted to your drinking."

"Yeah. We talked about that, too. He knows that I'm not drinking more than I used to. It's just the medication making me feel more drunk than I am. We agreed that I will try to drink less in the future."

"How do you feel about that?"

"Honestly, not great. It's been my crutch in social situations for a while now. It was probably the only reason I could talk to Nate in the first place. But he convinced me to try to see if the medication is working on its own without trying to self-medicate with alcohol."

"Do you think you'll be able to do that?"

"I'm going to try. If Celexa can help me be normal while sober, that would be amazing. I would like to see if I can, and if I can't, I know where to find the booze."

Stacey smiles. "Gemma, just be careful."

"I know. Drinking is bad while on medication."

"You said there was a lot going on other than this? Anything you'd like to talk about?"

"Yes! I met my new vice president, and I also applied for a new job."

"That's great news! Tell me about your meeting with the vice president first. Did you ask about working from home?"

"I didn't even have to. She brought it up. It's like she knew."

"She was open to you working from home full-time?"

"Yes and no. She is fine with me working from home two days a week. But if I want to work from home full-time, I need to talk to HR about an ADA accommodation."

"I see. Will you be asking for an accommodation? I will definitely write you a letter if they require one."

"Thank you. But I think I am going to see how things unfold in the next couple of weeks. Hopefully, I will be getting a new job. I want to see if that job is any better for my anxiety before I make any decisions about the accommodation."

"That's great, Gemma. How did applying go? Have you interviewed yet?"

"Ah, it went okay. I told Carl I wanted to apply, and he got sad and told me I didn't have to be a project manager. The interview, I don't know. I was probably really anxious and awkward, so I more than likely didn't get the job."

"Don't say that. I'm sure you are too hard on yourself. It probably wasn't nearly as bad as you think it was. Do you know if anyone else applied?"

"I don't know if anyone internal applied, but there were a couple of external applicants."

"You must have a leg up on them."

"I don't know. I was pretty awkward. I must have made them uncomfortable with my weirdness."

"Gemma, we need to work on how you see yourself versus what other people see."

Nah, I'd rather not.

"When do you know if you got the job?" Stacey asks.

"They said sometime this week, but who knows."

"I'm really excited for you, Gemma."

"Thank you."

"Was there anything else happening?"

"Oh, yeah. I got into a fight with Liz, and Nick and Brittany are getting together."

"Okay, that's a lot to unpack. Let's start with Liz. What happened there?"

"I had canceled on her a couple times for legitimate reasons, or so I thought, and I ended up telling her that I didn't think that seeing each other every single Saturday was sustainable."

"She did not take it well, I gather?"

"No. She did not. She told me that she could excuse me canceling on her for mental or medical reasons, but these last few weeks have been, and I quote, 'just me.'"

"Ouch. Do you think she's being unreasonable?"

"Yes. I was coming back from Foxwoods one week. I had to go out with Nate's parents the next. Oh, and to top it off, I canceled last weekend for Friendsgiving at Walter's. Though, I did ask her if she wanted to come, but she said no. I am pretty sure she would have canceled on me anyway that day. She still seems pretty cold to me."

"Have you talked to her about the fight or tried to reconcile with her since?"

"No. She hasn't talked to me. She just got up and walked out of Flannery's."

"I think she is feeling cut out of your life. She has a right to be upset, but I don't think that she acted fairly towards you. I believe she might be over reacting, but she does have a case for you being out of reach."

Damn. I hate when she skewers me like this. Okay, okay. Liz has a point.

"But what can I do about it? I told her I still wanted to see her, but it wouldn't be every single Saturday. I don't know what else to do."

"Give her some time to cool down and then ask her what she would like. And I want you to know, that even though I think she has a point, she is treating you unfairly. She shouldn't be acting like this."

Damn straight. She got so mad.

"Thank you. Yes. When she calms down, I will see what she wants to do."

"Good. And maybe have some alternative options, like seeing each other on a weekday night instead of Saturday if you can't make it on the weekend. So, she knows you still want to see her."

"Yeah, that's a good idea."

I hope Liz thinks so, too.

"Good. Do you want to talk about Nick and Brittany, in the time we have left?"

"Ugh. They are going to start dating. I can sense it. I already feel like I am being pushed out of the pack. Maybe not pushed out, but I'm definitely becoming the third wheel. I don't like it. It's uncomfortable. I don't know what to do or say when they are flirting and I don't exist. It makes me not want to hang out with them anymore."

"I see."

Oh, I hate when she says "I see" and then just stops talking. Sure, she sees, but I definitely don't see what she sees.

"Have you talked to them about it?"

"Not yet."

"You should. And may I note, don't get upset, that what you are feeling about Nick and Brittany, may be similar to what Liz is feeling about you and Nate."

Ah, shit. I hate when she drops knowledge on me like that.

CHAPTER FIFTEEN

Oh, it's arrived. It's finally arrived. Thank goodness it didn't take all week.

A meeting invite entitled "Interview Follow-up" has just popped into my inbox. The meeting is this morning with Roger right before lunch. Oh boy, I am equally excited and scared.

Why is my reaction to everything feeling like I'm going to throw up? That doesn't seem fair. Am I happy? Let's vomit. Am I sad? Let's barf. Am I anxious? Let's puke big time.

Thank goodness the meeting is today. If it were for another day, I don't think I'd survive the wait.

Roger is standing with his back to me and looking out the window when I enter the room and close the door.

"Gemma," he says. "Thanks for coming."

Oh, no. It's a no. Why would he thank me for coming if it's not a no?

He's just being polite. Now sit down.

Taking a seat across from him, I put the pen and pad of paper I brought with me down on the table.

Why the hell did you bring paper? Did you think you'd need to take notes and send out minutes after?

Maybe. You never know. Plus, it's weird going into a meeting with absolutely nothing. Who does that?

"I was really happy to get to know you better," Roger says.

Oh, shit. It's definitely a no.

"I've only worked with you on a few projects, but everyone I talk to thinks very highly of you."

Which is why he regrets to inform me that I am not getting the job?

"Which is why I…"

Oh, God. I was right. Here it comes.

"…am very happy to offer you the position on my team."

Yes!! I did it! I got the job!

"Really?" I ask.

Yes, really. Why would he joke about that? Honestly, Gemma, why did you ask that? He must think you're a fool now.

"Yes. Would you like time to think about it?" he asks.

"No."

"No?"

Oh, my God, Gemma. He thinks you are refusing the job. What is your problem? Say something. Tell him you're not rejecting the offer.

"No, I don't need time to think. I would like the job, yes."

"Okay, good. You had me worried for a second."

Well, get used to it. That will happen constantly now that I'm your employee. But you'll figure that out soon enough.

"So," he continues and slides a piece of paper across the table to me. "This is what your new salary will be."

He pauses for a moment while I turn over the paper and self-consciously look at the number without seeming like I am actually looking at the number, even though he was the one who told me to look at it.

What is wrong with you? Be normal.

I can't. Obviously.

Holy shit. This is a raise. I'm getting a raise! I'm getting a ten percent raise! Woohoo!

"And if you accept that, I will have to talk to Carl, but you will probably start in two weeks."

Of course, I accept! I'd be dumb not to.

Well…

Shut up!

Gemma! Answer!

"Yes, I accept. Thank you."

"Great! I'm so happy to hear that. I think you are going to be a great addition to our team."

Oh, yeah, baby. Moving out of the business analyst world and into the data warehouse developer world. No more leading project meetings. No more meetings where people pick apart my requirements. No more having to talk to Jack!

Well, you may still have to talk to him.

Shut up! Not as much. And I won't be leading the meeting or needing to get any information from him. I will just be an innocent bystander witnessing whatever torture he is inflicting on someone else.

"Do you have any questions for me?" Roger asks.

"Will I get any training?"

"Yes. We will probably sign you up for an online SQL course or two. And you will sit with Ed for a day or two to get the hang of things. But since you already know our data so well, I think that you will get up to speed very quickly, which is another reason I am glad you wanted the job."

"Will I have to move my desk?"

What kind of idiot question is that?

I like my desk.

"I'm not sure just yet. We may move you into Larry's old desk. But that reminds me, Jaqueline did mention that you expressed interest in continuing to work from home part-time. She was onboard with it. Honestly, I don't see an issue with it either. I know you are a great worker, and I'm sure you will be up and running in no time at all. We will just have you in the office full-time while you are new and training. But I expect within a month or two we should be able to get you working independently enough so that you can be remote a couple days a week."

Holy shit! I think I'm in love with Jaqueline. McGruff won't mind if I dump him for her, right? We can have a nice spring wedding. I absolutely adore her. She took my input and ran with it, ran completely away.

Just like you usually do.

Very funny. But she was running in a good way.

Yes, but you left her hanging on the ADA accommodation.

Well, I have a new job now. And I must be in the office full-time, so I will see how things go and revisit that again soon.

When you hate your job again?

Let's hope that doesn't happen.

"Gemma? Is that okay with you?"

Ah, shit. I always forget to answer.

"Yes, absolutely. I really appreciate it, especially since I am a new employee."

Okay, reign it in a little.

"I don't consider you a new employee. I know you. We all know you and what your work ethic is and what you will bring to this position. Jaqueline really wants to make KPM inclusive, and I am fully onboard with that."

Do you think she told him about your anxiety?

I don't know. Maybe. Or maybe he just has eyes and has seen me before.

Returning to my desk, I have two messages on my work chat and one text waiting for me. I sigh. Nothing from Liz.

Just text her. It will be fine. She is still your best friend. She will be happy for you.

I don't know.

She will. I promise.

I type up a message, "Hey. I know we haven't talked in a while, but you are the first person I want to tell. I got the job. And I was wondering if you want to celebrate with me on Saturday?"

Staring at my phone for a minute, my finger hovers over the send button.

Do it. She will be happy and say yes.

What if she isn't? What if she doesn't? What if she doesn't even respond?

Gemma! Of course, she will. She is Liz.

Taking a big breath, I hit the send button before letting it out.

Now we wait.

But it's only a few minutes before I get a response back.

"Yay! I knew you would! Of course, I do!"

My eyes start to well with tears.

No. What is this? Why are my eyes doing this?

Because you missed her, you idiot. And you were worried that you lost her.

I am so glad that I didn't.

"Oh, no," Brittany says as she appears and stands in front of my desk.

I hear Nick get up from his seat and see him immediately pop up next to Brittany.

"Oh, no, Gemma, I thought for sure you'd get the job," he says.

They both look at me with empathetic eyes.

"No," I blubber. "Happy tears."

Their eyes light up, and they both smile.

"Yes! I knew it!" Brittany says.

"You really had me there," Nick replies.

"Pack lunch!" Brittany declares.

"I'll invite Nate," Nick says.

"You will?" Brittany and I ask at the same time.

"Yeah, we are buds now. Why is that weird?"

Is it weird?

"No," I respond. "It would be less weird if I invited him, though. But feel free."

Brittany laughs.

"Fine, you invite him," Nick mumbles.

Taking out my phone, I type, "Pack lunch?" and hit send.

I get an immediate response. "Obviously." And then a quick follow up. "So did you get it?"

I type back, "Obviously."

"Woohoo!" he responds.

"Shall we?" Nick asks Brittany who is still next to him.

Our trio becomes a quad when McGruff finds us in the lobby. Before I can even say anything, he wraps his arms around me in a huge bear hug.

"That's my girl," he says. "My beautiful, brilliant girl. I am so happy for you." He pulls back and smiles at me. "My first pack lunch!"

"Yeah!" Nick says.

"Where to?" McGruff asks.

"Gemma's choice," Brittany says.

"Do you even have to ask?" I respond.

"Sally's it is," Brittany replies.

"Oh, good, I've been craving her mac and cheese," McGruff says.

"It's the best!" Nick responds, and the two of them take off in front of Brittany and me.

She and I look at each other. "Again with this," Brittany says and points to the guys, already at the doors to the building.

"At least, we have each other," I say.

Catching up to them right outside the doorway, we see the guys have waited and they hold the door for us to exit into the autumn air. They graciously continue to walk at our pace to Sally's for a total of thirty seconds before involuntarily speeding up without us.

Turning to look at Brittany, I say, "It's okay. Nick still likes you more than Nate. Nate is just new."

"I know."

"You know?" I ask. "What don't I know?"

"We are hanging out this weekend," she responds and smiles.

"Like a date?"

"He didn't say the word date, but I think so."

"Yay! That is awesome!"

"Yeah, hopefully it goes well."

"Of course, it will!"

"You must text me everything afterwards."

"Don't worry, I will."

We stop chatting when we catch up to the guys, who are waiting outside of Sally's. As we ding through the door, I see Walter sitting at the table by the window.

"Walter!" I say running over to him. "I got the job!"

"Oh, I'm so happy for you! Congratulations!" he says.

"Congrats, honey!" Sally shouts from behind the counter.

"Thanks, Sally!"

I sit opposite Walter, and Brittany sits next to me. Nick and McGruff order at the counter, wait for four plates of mac and cheese, and carry them over to the table.

"I can make room," Walter says. "I don't want to be in the way."

"Never," McGruff and I say at the same time.

McGruff winks at me as he drags a chair over from another table.

"I need to spend as much time as I can with you before you leave for New York City," I say to Walter.

"I have a couple of hours until then."

"That's not what I mean," I reply.

"I know, kid. I'll tell you what, I may drag my feet on that, too," he says and winks at me.

Yes! Don't get my hopes up.

"Walter," I say, "these are my friends Brittany and Nick."

You said friends. Not coworkers.

"I've heard a lot about you two," Walter replies.

"I've heard so much about you," Brittany responds.

"Where's Josh?" McGruff asks.

"He's at the apartment working and packing. He never really lets himself have time off."

Walter shakes his head.

"What are you doing to celebrate?" Sally asks. Walking over to the table, she stands and leans against the table next to us.

"Going out with Liz on Saturday," I say.

"See! I told you it would all work out," Walter says.

"I hope so."

"That's awesome," McGruff says.

"Where are you going?" Sally asks. "Same place as always?"

"Yep."

Sally slowly nods and looks at McGruff, who seems to nod back.

What was that look?

Has he been talking to Sally about my drinking, too?

No, you must be imagining things.

I'm just really glad that Liz wants to celebrate with me. I don't know what I would do without her in my life.

Let's just hope that she's forgiven you and this is not some ploy to get you there just to humiliate you or publicly berate you.

What! Why in the world would she do that?

You're right. She wouldn't. But let's just hope.

Okay, now I am worried.

"I'm nervous," I text to McGruff from the backseat of my Road Trip headed to see Liz Saturday night.

"Why?" he responds.

"I haven't seen Liz in weeks. I am worried it's going to be awkward."

"It will be fine. She's your best friend."

I sigh. Maybe. If she'll still have me.

Whoa girl, cheer up. This is a celebration.

"Will you be across the street so I can come see you if it gets weird?"

"First of all, it won't be weird. Second, no I am not going to O'Brady's tonight."

Damn it all to hell. Now what am I going to do if it all goes to shit?

It won't. Calm down.

Yeah, I'll just go home. No big deal.

The car stops in front of Flannery's, and I sigh once more.

How long can I wait here before the driver kicks me out? *Will* he kick me out? Will he *physically* kick me out?

Just get out of the car, Gemma!

Fine. Fine.

I open the car door and step onto the sidewalk. I've barely closed the door before the car speeds away.

Well, I guess that settles that. He definitely would have kicked me out.

Slowly stepping forward and steeling my nerves for what could be a cold reception from Liz, I pull open the door to the bar and step inside as I look at the floor.

"Surprise!"

Startled, my heart stops and my head snaps up.

What in the world?

There is a crowd of people starting at me, smiling, and clapping. What the shit is this? This can't be for me. Should I turn around and leave? I think that is the appropriate response here. I should turn around and hightail it out of here. This can't be for me.

But it is. Look. Look at the people.

There's Liz, Brett, McGruff, Brittany, Nick, Ed, McGruff's friends, Sally, and some other people from KPM. This can't be right. Why are they all here?

"Gemma! You coming in or what?" Liz shouts.

Or what. Definitely or what.

I haven't moved an inch. I am barely inside the door. Could this possibly be for me?

Are you dumb? Of course, this is for you! These are your friends and coworkers. Why wouldn't this be for you?

But why would it?

Gemma, seriously. Go in. Take a step forward. Do it.

And I do. I slowly take a few steps forward before the crowd descends upon me.

Liz is first. I hesitate for a moment before she hugs me.

"Oh, my God. I was so scared that you hated me forever," I say into her hair.

"I could never. I just needed some time to cool off and think. And you're right. Every Saturday is not sustainable. But we can talk about that later."

"I missed you."

"I missed you too."

"So much."

"Congrats on the new job," she says as we step apart. "I knew you'd be surprised."

"Definitely am."

She smiles as I hug Brittany and Nick and everyone else who has come out to Flannery's. McGruff is last.

"You knew about this," I say.

"Of course, I did."

"And you still let me panic about Liz?"

"Of course, I did."

I shake my head. "Horrible," is all I can get out before he kisses me.

"I love you," he says.

My heart flutters like the first time I looked into those hypnotizing baby blue eyes.

"I love you, too."

Leaning down, he kisses my forehead, and we turn to look at all of the people who came out to celebrate my new job.

"Drink?" he asks.

"Nah. I got this."

"You sure?"

Why does he have to test my resolve like that? He knows I'll crack under pressure.

"Maybe just one."

He slips his hand into mine, and I lean my head on his shoulder. My friends are here. My coworkers are here.

Your coworkers that happen to be friends.

My friends that happen to be coworkers.

I've got a new job. I've got McGruff by my side. Life is good.

Did you just say that?

Yes, yes I did. Life is good.